*Elizabeth and Tom are at
war . . . and in love.*

"Between you and Jessica, there is no tactic too low," Elizabeth lashed out. "I can't believe you would use my own sister to pump me for information! And I know what you're doing with Dana—trying to make me jealous. I guess you think I'm so desperate to get you back, I'll turn over all my notes."

"No," Tom began. "You've got me all wrong. Well . . . OK, some of it you have right. But I'm not out to get you. Really. I'm not."

"Yes, you are," she insisted. "I don't need you anymore, and you can't stand it."

"All right. Have it your way. You don't need me. But I need you."

Elizabeth's heart banged hard inside her chest, then skipped a beat. She let out a cry. "No," she choked. "Please . . . don't say anything else." Elizabeth didn't want to hear any more—because in spite of everything that had been said and done, she still wanted to believe him. And every time she believed him, she wound up getting hurt.

Tom stepped toward her. "I need you," he continued, ignoring her pleas. "Not just to help me get this story. I need you to be happy. I miss you."

Bantam Books in the Sweet Valley University series.
Ask your bookseller for the books you have missed.

And don't miss these Sweet Valley
University Thriller Editions:

Visit the Official Sweet Valley Web Site on the Internet at:

http://www.sweetvalley.com

SWEET VALLEY UNIVERSITY®

Undercover Angels

Written by
Laurie John

Created by
FRANCINE PASCAL

BANTAM BOOKS
NEW YORK · TORONTO · LONDON · SYDNEY · AUCKLAND

RL 8, age 14 and up

UNDERCOVER ANGELS
A Bantam Book / December 1997

Sweet Valley High® *and Sweet Valley University*®
are registered trademarks of Francine Pascal.
Conceived by Francine Pascal.
Produced by Daniel Weiss Associates, Inc.
33 West 17th Street
New York, NY 10011.

ISBN: 0-553-57059-5

Published simultaneously in the United States and Canada

Bantam Books are published by Bantam Books, a division of Bantam Doubleday Dell Publishing Group, Inc. Its trademark, consisting of the words "Bantam Books" and the portrayal of a rooster, is Registered in U.S. Patent and Trademark Office and in other countries. Marca Registrada. Bantam Books, 1540 Broadway, New York, New York 10036.

PRINTED IN THE UNITED STATES OF AMERICA

OPM   0 9 8 7 6 5 4 3 2 1

To Bara Joy Colodne

Chapter
One

"Mack the Hack!" Bruce Patman fumed over breakfast. "That's what Anderson called me yesterday afternoon. *Mack the Hack!*"

Bruce put on his Ray-Ban sunglasses, not to shield his eyes against the Wednesday morning sunlight that streamed through the University Center windows but to get himself into the character of supersnob Anderson Pettigrew. He slouched over, letting his broad shoulders droop like Anderson's thin bony ones. "Oh, Paaahhhtman," he drawled, imitating Anderson's been-there-done-that-rich-kid voice. "Have you heard what the VIPs are calling you? 'Maaahhhck the Haaahhhck.'"

Bruce punctuated his imitation with a long, drawn-out whinny of a giggle. Proud of his impersonation, he removed his sunglasses with flair and waited for Lila Fowler's appreciative laugh.

But the love of Bruce's life looked less than amused.

1

"Oh, shut up," Lila snapped as she flipped through the pages of her red leather-bound address book. "I am *so* sick of listening to you obsess over this."

"Obsess!" Bruce yelped, stung. "Considering that I was willing to make a total fool of myself for your sake—correction. Considering that *you* were willing to make a total fool out of *me* on the off chance that the Verona Springs Country Club VIPs *might* let you join their elite little circle, I'd think you could at least show me a tiny bit of sympathy."

"I don't have time for sympathy, and you don't have time for self-pity. Now sit down and make yourself useful. Help me address these thank-you notes." She pushed a little stack of cream-colored monogrammed envelopes across the table. "Since Pepper Danforth chose *me* to organize the Verona Springs VIP Mixed Doubles Tournament, I want to send one to every person who participated. And I want to do it on *my* stationery so they'll know *exactly* who was in charge."

"If you think you were in charge," Bruce retorted, "you're kidding yourself. *I'll* tell you who was in charge—Paul Krandall and Bunny Sterling, that's who. They're the ones who walked off with that cheap trophy last night—just like they do every year. And besides, the Verona Springs Snob Squad should be thanking *you*. You went to a lot of trouble to organize their crummy tournament. You went to a lot of trouble to make sure I threw the match so Paul and Bunny could win. And you set me up so Paul could hustle me later." He let out a snort of disgust. "They should give you the VIP Medal for Exceptional Finkery, Lila."

"Stop being so snide. Organizing that tournament was a big job. It was an *honor* to be asked to do it. Pepper said it was a test of my *organizational ability.*"

Bruce rolled his eyes. "If you ask me, it was a test of your *kiss-up* ability."

Lila's brown eyes sizzled. "Take that back!" she demanded.

"No! That tournament was a farce. You know it and I know it. And the funny part is, I was actually looking *forward* to playing in it. What a laugh!" Bruce smiled weakly. "That was before I knew you were going to beat me black and blue by swiping at my ankles and . . . and anything else you could reach with your racket."

"What else could I do?" Lila squeaked. "You kept scoring points. I had to stop you. We were going to win, and beating Paul Krandall is *certain social suicide.* How many times do I have to tell you?" She let out an exasperated groan.

"I wonder if Pepper was in on Paul's hustling scam," Bruce muttered. "I still can't believe I fell for it. The oldest trick in the book. He walks around pretending he's got the IQ of an eggplant and the serve of a C-minus player, and the whole time he's setting up marks."

"So you're an easy mark," Lila murmured. "What's new?"

"I should have smelled a rat when he challenged me to that private rematch yesterday morning—on the *back* court—so we could play 'privately.' What he really meant was *with no witnesses.*" Bruce shook his head remorsefully. "There I was, thinking I was heading for an easy win, and suddenly he started slamming aces like Pete Sampras! Do you have *any* idea how much money he won off me?"

Lila shrugged as if she really didn't much care. "Paul made fools out of both of us. You don't hear me complaining, do you? Besides, when you went out with Bunny, you treated her like dirt. Paul's her fiancé. He had a duty to avenge her. He *did*. So take it like a man and quit whining."

Bruce got up and paced around the table, his hands shoved down into the pockets of his khakis. "Gee, thanks. I appreciate your sympathy. The entire country club thinks Bruce Patman can't return a serve now—but hey, don't worry. Whatever makes you happy, darling."

"Obsessing," Lila sang under her breath as she scratched the nib of her expensive fountain pen across a thick note card. "He's obsessing."

"I'm not obsessing! I'm *venting*. There's a difference."

Lila put down her pen and turned in her chair to look at him. A smile played at the corner of her mouth, and Bruce's heart thumped. It was amazing that Lila Fowler could do that to him. They'd known each other since the sixth grade and hated each other until this year. He was a college sophomore. She, a freshman. When she had turned up on the Sweet Valley University campus, they had seen each other through new eyes and fallen for each other—hard. They were perfect for each other too. Lila Fowler was one of the richest girls in California. Bruce had come into his trust fund this year and had almost as much—maybe more?—money than she did. They both loved expensive things and could both afford the best.

But just because Bruce had a lot of money didn't mean he wanted to be cheated. It didn't mean he wanted to join some dorky country club for well-to-do college couples either. For the life of him, he couldn't figure out what Lila saw in that crowd. "What are you smiling at?" he asked grumpily.

"You," Lila answered, lowering her eyelids flirtatiously. "You're so cute when you're being unreasonable and childish." Her eyes shone behind dark fringes of expensively tinted eyelashes. She had them dyed once a week at The Eyes Have It, a salon for eyebrows and lashes only. Lila had a standing appointment once a week to which Bruce accompanied her in case something hurt and she wanted her hand held. Bruce teased her about it, but it was time and money well spent. Her eyes were incredibly beautiful.

Bruce threw himself into the chair beside hers. Even though she was looking aggressively tempting, he wasn't quite ready to be teased out of his tantrum. He was having too much fun ridiculing her "friends"—Pepper Danforth, with her fried platinum blond hair and plastic fingernails, and her too-jaded boyfriend, Anderson. And all the other overdressed, underclassed Verona Springs VIPs. "I'm not being child—"

"Yes, you are," she said abruptly. "You complain that the VIPs are rich snobs. But you're a rich snob too."

"Am not," he retorted.

"Are too," she insisted. "I'm not judging. Who am I to judge? I'm a rich snob and happy to be one. *And* I want to be in the Verona Springs VIP Circle too. It's my goal, OK? You're my boyfriend. You're supposed to help me achieve my goal. So stop 'venting' and *help me*."

"Lila! A *goal* is putting a man on the moon or increasing productivity twenty percent. Getting into the Verona Springs VIP Circle is not a *goal*. It's . . . it's . . ." He racked his brains, searching for the right word.

"It's what I *want*," she said simply.

Bruce sighed and stared down at the toes of his beige-and-sand-colored nubuck oxfords. Well, that was that.

Game over!

Checkmate!

Bingo!

Gin!

Meeting adjourned!

Because on Planet Lila, that was just the way things were. If Lila wanted it, it was Bruce's job to see that she got it.

Lila leaned close until her eyes and lips were less than two inches from his. Bruce's heart began to hammer in his chest. "You want me to be happy, don't you?" she asked in her low, throaty voice.

He closed his eyes. Why did he ever try to argue with Lila? It was futile. Pointless. He loved her madly and insanely. She drove him up the wall, across the ceiling, and down the other side. But he always came back for more.

He felt the pressure of her lips against his, and a slow flutter of electricity moved up and down his spine. One of these days he was going to have to get a grip and quit knuckling under. Let Lila know she couldn't use him like a garden implement to do her dirty work.

Not now, though.

He opened one eye and peered at his watch. Darn. It was later than he thought, and he needed to get to the bank as soon as it opened. He pulled away reluctantly. "I've got to go. I've got to make sure I have enough money in my account to cover the check I wrote Paul after our 'rematch.'"

Lila pushed him away so hard, he fell out of his chair. "Hurry!" she urged. "Whatever you do, don't write him a hot check. Not after you tried to sic the police on him."

Bruce flushed scarlet. She *would* bring that up.

Elizabeth Wakefield left her eight o'clock biology class and walked quickly through the long hallway of the life sciences building and out the front door into the sunlight.

Students hurried in every direction—laughing, talking, walking, and in-line skating. Behind the Sweet Valley University center, miles beyond the campus, mountains hovered on the horizon like purple-and-green shadows.

Elizabeth quickened her step, her mind busily sketching out her day. She had a lot to do, but priority one was working on her story for the *Sweet Valley Gazette*. *And what a story it's turning out to be!* she thought. It wasn't a nice story, but it was shaping up to be major.

When Elizabeth had been assigned to write a puff piece on the Verona Springs Country Club for the student paper, she'd been more than a little peeved. Even though she was only a freshman, she'd already established a name for herself in the world of hard-hitting student journalism with her reporting for WSVU, the campus television station. She didn't appreciate being assigned to squishy society stories. And unlike her identical twin sister, Jessica, she didn't enjoy hanging around country clubs, sorority houses, hip restaurants, and trendy boutiques.

Jessica! That was a whole other mess entirely. Elizabeth quickened her step, agitated at the memory of spotting Jessica at the country club disguised as someone named Perdita with her hair dyed jet-black. *I wasn't sure which one of us had lost her mind,* she recalled with a nervous giggle. Jessica had eventually revealed that she was working undercover with her boyfriend, Nick Fox, a police detective. But she had refused to tell Elizabeth why.

Elizabeth was pretty sure she knew the answer. In researching her piece, Elizabeth had discovered an article about an incident that had taken place at the club just a couple of weeks ago. Dwayne Mendoza, an SVU student working at the club as a caddy, had been found floating in the Verona Springs Reservoir. Possibly murdered. *Probably* murdered. The story had been virtually buried, and Elizabeth's journalistic radar screamed "cover-up."

When she and her partner, Scott Sinclair, arrived

at Verona Springs, she'd started digging around and asking questions, but everything came up empty. Just when she'd been wondering if her radar was on the fritz, she'd run into Tom Watts in the garden maze. That confirmed her instincts were right on target.

Tom was the anchor reporter for WSVU—and her ex-boyfriend. He wouldn't have been there if there wasn't a story. She and Tom had begun talking—arguing, actually—when suddenly a gardener approached them, warned them to be very, very careful, and hurried away. Elizabeth had pursued him and discovered that he was the uncle of the dead caddy. He'd mentioned the word *murder*. Then he disappeared. When Elizabeth had returned to the club the next day to question him further, she had been told that he retired. In Elizabeth's mind that translated into foul play.

The thought that something might have happened to the elderly gardener pierced her heart with the same intensity she felt whenever she thought of Tom Watts. "Oh, Tom," she whispered. "Why can't we put everything aside and work together on this?"

She knew why all too well. There had been a time when Tom and Elizabeth had been a top-notch team—professionally and personally. But those days were over now. Ever since Tom's newfound biological father, George Conroy, had made a pass at her. Elizabeth had confided in Tom, but he hadn't believed her. Instead Tom had lashed out at her for being jealous and trying to destroy his happiness. They'd broken up—and he'd been nothing but cruel to her ever since. There were times when she'd think she saw a spark of love in his eyes, but inevitably he'd turn vicious and break her heart all over again.

Suppressing a wave of tears, she tightened her long blond ponytail and reminded herself that the man she had once loved was now her fiercest competitor. So now, no matter what, she was determined to beat him to the finish line. *All's fair in love, war, and reporting,* she thought. *So watch your back, Watts.*

She turned her attention from her ex-boyfriend to the story at hand. With a surge of pride she remembered how Tom had mistakenly led her to another fact: Another caddy, Brandon Phillips, had been found in possession of some of Mendoza's belongings and was being held by police for questioning about his death. Her partner, Scott, had called the police two days ago and discovered that Phillips was still being held. Surely that meant the police had charged Phillips with murder. But *something* told Elizabeth that Phillips was the wrong guy.

"Hey, Liz! Liz!" she heard someone call, snapping her out of her thoughts. She looked up and saw Bruce Patman walking toward her, waving.

"Good morning," she called out.

"Morning."

Elizabeth smothered a chuckle. She had known Bruce Patman since middle school, and he had always been a big egomaniac. He'd looked pretty silly the last time she saw him, though—angrily telling two policemen that he had been robbed by Paul Krandall.

He fell into step beside her. "I never got a chance

to talk to you about that Paul Krandall thing," he began. "I know you're writing about the Verona Springs VIPs. Right? How about an exclusive interview with an unnamed source about a hustling scam going on there?"

Elizabeth laughed. "Why do you want to be an unnamed source?" she asked.

"Because Lila will *kill* me if she catches me bad-mouthing any of those VIPs," Bruce replied with a scowl. "Joining the VIP Circle is her new goal. And you know how Lila gets when anyone steps in her way."

"Hmmm," Elizabeth murmured. "I'd think you would have had enough anonymity by now."

Bruce blushed. "All right. All right. I didn't handle that very well. You don't have to rub it in. But I thought the press was supposed to be on the side of the truth."

Elizabeth remembered the scene—the police car driving up to the front parking lot just as Paul came walking out. Responding to an anonymous tip, they had come to investigate a robbery supposedly committed by Paul Krandall. They had searched Paul's bag and removed a huge wad of cash. Paul quickly explained he hadn't *stolen* the money, he had *won* it. From Bruce Patman.

The police had paged Bruce Patman inside the clubhouse. When Bruce came out into the parking lot, the police asked him if he had indeed lost a large sum of money to Paul. When Bruce replied that he had and that *he* had called the police, the police angrily threatened to run Bruce in for filing a false police report. Losing a bet wasn't

11

the same as "being robbed," they'd told him.

"I still say I was hustled," Bruce insisted.

"Hmmm," Elizabeth murmured again.

"You don't believe me, do you? You just think I'm a bad player and a sore loser. If you or anybody else had seen that second match, you'd realize I was scammed."

Elizabeth raised her eyebrows in mock surprise. Bruce wasn't much of a sport. He was the type who would always cry foul when he lost. Elizabeth had watched him in the mixed doubles tournament. He was a terrible player. Even when she and Scott had played— and lost—the previous afternoon, they hadn't even been a fraction as awful as Bruce and Lila. Bruce should have known better than to play anybody for money.

"I don't care what you think," Bruce muttered. "If it weren't for Lila, I'd stop payment on that check instead of trying to cover it."

Elizabeth skidded to a stop. *Check?*

Bruce stopped beside her. "What's the matter?"

"Did you say you wrote Paul a check?" she asked.

Bruce nodded. "Yeah."

"You didn't give him cash?" she pressed, remembering the large wad of cash in the policeman's hand.

"Are you kidding? Who carries that much cash around?" Bruce asked.

Good question, Elizabeth thought.

Bruce veered off. "Gotta go. I have to be at the bank when it opens. If that check bounces . . ."

Elizabeth watched Bruce trot away, her mind in a whirl. If Bruce hadn't paid Paul in cash, where had that big wad of money come from? And why had

Paul pretended to the police that the cash in his possession was money he had won from Bruce?

"I've got to tell Scott about this," she whispered, turning on her heel and heading for the *Gazette* offices. Sure enough, just as she approached the steps Scott Sinclair came walking out with another reporter she had seen around. "Hi," Elizabeth said, waving.

"Hey, you," Scott replied gently, a sweet smile lighting up his handsome face.

Elizabeth shifted in place uneasily. Ever since they'd met, Scott had always been a little more demonstrative toward her than she appreciated. She had to admit he was gorgeous, with his shoulder-length blond hair and crystalline blue eyes, but she could never feel fully relaxed around him—especially now that their assignment at the country club required them to pose as a couple. He'd tried to carry the act back to campus with them countless times, but she'd always resisted.

Why am I holding back? she wondered, admiring how perfectly put together he looked in his crisp white oxford and well-worn blue jeans. *He's smart, he's good-looking . . .*

. . . but he's not Tom Watts, a taunting voice in her head supplied. Clearing her throat, she pushed the thought aside and offered her hand to the other reporter. "Hi, we've never actually met. I'm Elizabeth Wakefield."

"I know," the young man replied with a friendly, lopsided smile. "Scott's told me all about you. Miko Oshima."

13

As they shook hands Elizabeth struggled to keep a smile on her face. She didn't even want to hazard a guess as to what Scott might have told Miko. *Is Scott telling the world we're dating when we're really not?* she wondered anxiously. But judging from Miko's appearance, with his shaved head, baggy chinos that dragged under his high tops, and battered T-shirt that read Skate and Destroy, he certainly wasn't the paper's gossip columnist. *Just relax,* she told herself. *It doesn't matter what Scott told Miko. All that matters is the story.*

"Listen, Scott," she began, hoping that Miko would excuse himself. This was her story, and the fewer people who knew about it, the better off she'd be. "I really need to talk to you—"

"I'm gonna take off," Miko said, obviously taking the hint. He reached into his pocket and handed Scott a set of keys. "Here you go, man. You sure you don't want to tell me why you need my van?"

Scott winked at Elizabeth. "You'll just have to wait and read about it in the paper like everybody else. Thanks for the loan, Miko. I'll get it back to you by tomorrow."

Miko lifted his hand and shambled off toward the dorms.

"I've got something to tell you," Elizabeth began once Miko was out of earshot. "About the money Paul Krandall had."

Scott reached into his pocket, pulled out his own set of keys, and handed them to Elizabeth.

"Tell me on the way to the parking lot. I need you to drive my car."

"Where are we going?" she asked. "And why *are* you borrowing Miko's van?"

"There's a reception this afternoon for Congressman Krandall—Paul Krandall's dad," Scott explained. "And I have this little idea. . . ."

Chapter Two

"'What will Paul do next?'" Tom Watts murmured, reading the headline of the latest edition of *Scene,* a weekly newspaper that chronicled the social life of Sweet Valley County. *Scene* was what was called an "insert" because it was circulated free inside the local daily newspaper, mainly as a way to publicize new restaurants and shops.

He smirked at the picture of Paul on the front page, holding the tennis trophy he and his girlfriend, Bunny Sterling, had won yesterday evening at the Verona Springs VIP Mixed Doubles Tournament.

Tom swiveled back and forth in his chair, his black loafers resting on top of his desk. *Paul Krandall does* not *look like a bright guy,* Tom decided, studying his round face and heavy-lidded eyes.

In the flesh Paul was even less impressive. Most of what he had to say was inane, and his attempts at humor were feeble. But Tom had seen with his own eyes that Paul did have a talent—at breaking into his own car. After Paul had enlisted Tom's help in opening the door to his Porsche, the keys locked inside, the belligerent dope had flipped up the inside latch with Tom's hanger in milliseconds.

Was Bruce right? Was Paul a hustler? Somebody who played dumb well enough to cheat anyone and rich enough to get away with it?

Tom had witnessed the ludicrous scene in the club parking lot. The questioning of Paul. The summoning of Bruce. The accusation of hustling. And then, after Bruce had withdrawn into the club, the return to Paul of an *extremely* large wad of cash. Money Paul claimed to have won from Bruce.

Whether or not Paul was the idiot he pretended to be was not, however, the most important question to Tom. What Tom wanted to know was, How had Paul wound up with a ten-dollar bill with the words *buena suerte* written on it?

When Tom had glimpsed the bill in the parking lot, he'd gasped out loud. He recognized that ten-dollar bill because *he* had written those words himself. While waiting for his sort-of girlfriend, Dana Upshaw, in the club employees' lounge, Tom had seen several members of the staff contribute to a collection taken up by Carlos, the headwaiter. Carlos had explained that a former employee was getting married. He'd said it was customary for coworkers to give a gift of cash.

Tom had offered to contribute too. Carlos had been reluctant to accept, but Tom had insisted. He

17

had written *buena suerte,* Spanish for good luck, on a ten-dollar bill and given it to Carlos. Carlos had thanked him and added the bill to the wad of cash he had collected. Somehow, it seemed, that money had ended up in Paul's hands.

Tom shook his head in confusion. *Elizabeth was in the parking lot too,* he told himself. *She probably saw the cash. What did she make of it? Knowing Elizabeth, she's probably already got a theory. And you, Watts, have squat!*

Tom swiveled harder in his chair, his heart sinking. If he were working with Elizabeth on this story, he'd know everything there was to know by now. They were magic together in every way.

"Elizabeth . . . how did I let you get away?" he moaned softly. "And how do I get you back?"

"Are you talking to yourself?" an amused voice asked.

Startled, Tom jerked his feet off the desk, sat up, and shoved the copy of *Scene* under his desk. Dana Upshaw was smiling at him from the door.

Tom gulped guiltily and felt his face turn red. He was pretty sure Dana hadn't been able to hear his words; she was smiling sexily as if she was very sure of her welcome.

"I guess I *was* talking to myself," Tom answered, pretending to busy himself at his desk. "Thinking out loud. A writer's habit."

"Do you have a second?"

"Absolutely. How's my favorite cellist?"

As she sauntered toward him he could smell the mysterious perfume that floated off her long mahogany

18

hair. Dana looked like a music major ought to look, he reflected. Her clothes were wild, sometimes outlandish, and always sexy. Today she wore a long, black, sleeveless tube dress that just met the toes of her combat boots and a choker that appeared to be made out of bones and leather. He did a double take when he saw a crudely rendered black heart decorating her left shoulder.

"I didn't know you had a tattoo," Tom remarked.

"It's Magic Marker, sweetie," she purred. "Thought it matched the outfit. It's called *accessorizing*."

"Oh." He shook his head as if to clear away the thought growing there: that Elizabeth Wakefield would never, ever, in a million years draw on herself to complement an outfit. Yet in spite of the fact that Tom often found himself with Elizabeth on his mind, his pulse always quickened when Dana got close. Like it was quickening right now.

Dana sat down on the edge of Tom's desk and ran her hand over the top of his computer. "What are you doing this afternoon?"

Realizing that his story notes were on the computer, he leaned forward and surreptitiously turned off the screen.

Dana smiled. "Oh, don't worry," she teased. "I'm not trying to find out your secrets. I'm just here to see if you want to go to a reception at Verona Springs this afternoon."

Tom suppressed a wince. He had originally invited Dana to hang with him at Verona Springs because many of the club's areas had a "couples-only" rule.

She had no idea he had needed her in order to investigate a possible murder. Tom felt slightly guilty about using her. He could live with it, though. Dana was eager to go anywhere with Tom, and she had managed to get *herself* some good out of it—a gig with the club's string quartet. "What's the occasion?" he asked.

"Congressman Krandall, Paul's father, is coming to town. It's probably a campaign stop. At any rate, the Verona Springs VIPs are having a little reception for him. The quartet's going to play, and I thought maybe you'd like to come."

"I'd love to," Tom answered, meaning it. "Maybe I can talk Congressman Krandall into giving me an interview."

"Tom!" Dana's lower lip protruded prettily. Tom couldn't help noticing the deep mauve color of her mouth. "How insulting! You're supposed to want to come so you can gaze at me. Not so you can talk to some stuffy old congressman."

Tom opened and closed his mouth while his brain moved into damage control mode. But when Dana threw back her head and laughed at her own exaggerated coyness, he realized she had been teasing. Tom laughed too—uneasily. He could never tell when Dana was pulling his leg. With Elizabeth, he always knew where the conversation was going.

A wave of remorse washed over him when he thought about Elizabeth. He'd had the greatest girl in the world, and he'd blown it. Tom resolutely pushed his feelings aside. He couldn't afford to give in to them now. He needed to keep Dana on the string at least until he finished his investigation. "I'd love to come and gaze at you," he told her, trying to match her teasing tone.

Dana reached forward and covered his hand with hers. "I'm happy to be getting so much of your time these days. Verona Springs has been really good for us. Don't you think?" Her voice was deep and throaty, and her eyes urged him to agree, to make some kind of declaration of mutual passion. But Tom's heart was still too full of Elizabeth, and he couldn't quite bring himself to lie.

"It's a nice club," he evaded, trying to keep his tone light. "I like going there. Good food. Tennis courts. Music. What's not to like?"

She cocked her head and studied him through seductive eyes. "Why do I have the feeling you're not being completely honest with me? I don't think the music or the facilities are what draw you to the club. And I *know* you're not interested in becoming a VIP." Her tone was still seductive and playful.

"You don't know that," he teased back, taking his tone from hers. "Maybe I do want to be a VIP. Hang out with Bunny and Paul. Pepper and Anderson. I know they seem superficial and not too bright. But sometimes people are more than they seem. What do you think? Any unplumbed depths there?"

It was a fishing trip. But Dana was a pretty sharp girl. There was no telling what she might have observed or overheard.

She shook her head. "I'm just a hired fiddle player. But if you ask me, what you see with those

21

guys is pretty much what you get. But you'll come anyway, right? It'll be a nice reception, and I'm going to play something new. Something just for you." She ran her hand down his sleeve. "Something romantic."

Tom swallowed self-consciously. When Dana came on this strong, it kind of unnerved him. "Great," he enthused. His voice came out higher than usual.

Dana smiled knowingly, as if she understood the effect she had on him. She floated to the door, her long, stretchy dress doing interesting things. "I have to be there early, so I'll drive over around lunchtime. You can meet me there when you get ready. See you later." The door closed behind her, and Tom caught a last whiff of her potent perfume.

Tom closed his eyes and breathed deeply. Dana might come on strong, but he had to admit it was nice to have a girl make it clear she thought he was a hero and not a creep. Nice to have a girl who wasn't accusing him of doing her dirty and scooping her story.

Speaking of which . . . Tom leaned forward, flipped on his screen, and studied his notes. There was a story there, all right. The only problem was, several chapters were missing. Chapters he hoped to fill in before Elizabeth and that slick-as-slime-Scott-guy-who-calls-himself-a-reporter-but-probably-couldn't-find-a-lead-story-in-a-library got to it first.

He sighed guiltily. Maybe Elizabeth had Tom pegged right all along. Maybe he *was* the creep she accused him of being.

There was no getting around it. He was using Dana in a way no nice guy would. And he *did* want

22

to scoop Elizabeth. Scoop her and then rub her nose in it if he could.

Why?

Because I'm nuts about her, that's why, he concluded with a moan.

Elizabeth sat in Scott's car in the parking lot of the PharValue Superstore and worriedly looked at her watch. Scott was late. What was taking so long?

A chain-link fence behind the superstore closed off the southern edge of the Verona Springs golf course. Some little kids clung to the fence, laughing and pushing each other. But Scott was nowhere in sight.

Maybe Scott should have invited Miko along, she thought anxiously. But both Elizabeth and Scott had agreed that it was better Miko not know anything except that they needed to borrow his van. That was then, however. Now she was more than a little scared.

Scott's plan was to drive the van to the country club, leave it in the parking lot early before people started to arrive, then cut across the golf course, climb the fence, and rendezvous with Elizabeth. That way if they wanted to follow anybody away from the reception, they could do it more effectively and anonymously in Miko's gray van than in Scott's taxi yellow convertible.

The morning sun was higher in the sky now, and it was getting hot inside the car. Elizabeth rubbed her damp palms against her jeans and shifted in her

23

seat. "Come on, come *on*," she urged under her breath. "Where *are* you?"

Beads of perspiration formed along her brow. A feeling of heavy dread settled around her shoulders. *Did somebody see Scott and—*

Elizabeth let out a sigh of relief when she spotted Scott coming over the chain-link fence with a Frisbee, much to the delight of the mischievous children in the parking lot. He smiled and gave them the Frisbee. Then he walked toward his car in a way that aroused no suspicion. *Scott's good,* Elizabeth thought. *Incredibly good.*

"I wouldn't have thought of the Frisbee," she told him as he opened the door and slid into the driver's seat. "Nice touch."

He acknowledged the compliment with a smile. "You know, anyone who saw me could figure, 'What a good guy. He went over the fence to get their Frisbee.' No Frisbee and they think, 'Look at that guy sneaking off the golf course. What was he up to?'"

"I'll remember that. It's a good trick," she said, her shoulders beginning to relax.

"OK," he said. "That's done. Now we go to the county records office."

"Did anybody see you?" she asked as he started the car.

"I don't think so," he answered, backing out. "There were a few cars in the club parking lot. Probably staff because there's nobody on the courts or the golf course yet."

"Did you see anything?" she asked.

He shook his head and grinned. "No. But it's not even ten o'clock yet. What's your rush?" He pulled out onto the highway. "Patience, Elizabeth. Patience. You'll need it at the county records office. It takes a while to get information."

Elizabeth took off her Windbreaker and stuffed it down into the seat beside her. "What about classes?" she asked. "I don't have any more today. But you've got three."

"Some things are more important than classes," he replied, turning on the blinker and accelerating onto the freeway.

Chapter
Three

"So *that's* how you do it!" Nick Fox watched, fascinated, as Jessica Wakefield painted on a mouth that looked nothing like her own in the middle of the Red Circle Diner, a place so grubby and run-down that none of the Verona Springs VIPs would possibly be caught dead there. She sat across from him in the booth, working with a small compact and a brush. She wielded the brush with small, deft strokes.

"Pretty amazing, huh?"

"Amazing," he agreed. "And slightly appalling. It's unnerving watching the girl I love morph herself into somebody else over breakfast. If you weren't working undercover, I'd beg you to take off that Perdita disguise and go back to being the Jessica Wakefield I adore."

"You say the sweetest things," she cooed sarcastically. "But don't think you can sweet-talk me off this case."

Nick scraped the last of his eggs off his plate and

laughed. Supposedly they were investigating a murder at the Verona Springs Country Club. But Nick felt more like he was playing undercover cop in order to humor Jessica. "It's not turning out to be much of a case," he pointed out. "Just as well. I'd hate to have you along on something really dangerous."

"I helped you before on a dangerous case."

He swallowed thoughtfully before replying, memories of the chop shop bust Jessica had floated into clogging his brain. "Yes. You did. But you almost got us killed too."

"I closed the case, baby," she insisted. "And don't you forget it."

"Beginner's luck. Don't get carried away. Take it slow."

"Chief Wallace wouldn't have told you to bring me in on this if he didn't think I could handle it."

Nick leaned back his head and laughed. "He told me to bring you because you're the country club type and I'm a clod who doesn't know a pickle fork from ice tongs. You're helping me blend in."

"Aha! So you *do* need me." Jessica smiled happily and examined her reflection again.

Nick knew that Jessica was always happy when she could force him to admit he needed her help. And in this situation he definitely did.

The only drawback was that the club seemed to be full of people who knew Jessica, including her twin sister, Elizabeth, and her best friend, Lila Fowler. Jessica had worked around that by disguising herself as a classy Argentinean heiress. She had dyed her long blond hair an alarming shade of jet-black. Instead of falling around her shoulders in loose waves, today it was held in a severe bun at the nape of her neck. She'd scoured vintage clothing stores for a lot of forties-style rayon dresses with big floral patterns. To complete her transformation, she wore big sunglasses and a filmy scarf around her head.

Nick had a hard time believing her "disguise" would fool anybody. But as it turned out, the members of the Verona Springs Country Club were so self-absorbed, they didn't notice much of anything. Besides, there was nothing to investigate as far as Nick was concerned—unless somebody had passed a law against snobbery. None of those Verona Springs VIPs had the brains, never mind the initiative, to commit any crime.

Jessica had finished outlining a large, full, forties-style mouth in black. Now she was filling in the lines with plum red lip gloss.

He reached forward and stayed her hand. "Jessica," he said seriously. "I'm glad you're having fun. And it's fun for me to be working with you on something. But I don't want you to be disappointed if the chief pulls the plug."

"Oh, Nick! Don't let him do that. Please."

Nick reached around and massaged the back of his neck. His leather jacket squeaked reassuringly. He'd had this jacket for years. He liked the way it sounded. He liked the way it smelled. It made him feel like Nick. Not "Chip," Perdita's preppy date. "So far all we've seen at the club is a bunch of uptight snobs, and all we've heard is their high-and-mighty babbling. If the chief asks me what we've found, I've got to tell him the truth. Nothing."

"What happens then?" she asked, her heavily darkened eyebrows meeting over her nose.

"I'll be reassigned to an active case, and you can . . ." He waved his hand, not quite sure exactly what it was that Jessica did when she wasn't with him. "You can go back to being blond—with a normal-looking mouth."

Jessica closed her compact with an irritated snap. She rocked slightly on her side of the booth, her platform shoes tapping ominously on the floor beneath the Formica table.

Nick sighed. "Jessica, I'm nuts about you, and I appreciate your help. But we're not getting anywhere. There's *nothing* going on. Nothing that warrants police investigation anyway."

"If there's nothing going on at the club, then why are Elizabeth and Tom so interested?" she demanded. "What are *they* sniffing around for?"

Nick leaned forward and raised his eyebrows. "I wish I knew," he said honestly. "I wish you could get them to tell me. Now *that* might help me."

Jessica's face fell, and she twisted the small brush in her hand. Nick watched the scarlet tip retract, feeling like a jerk. No real rookie cop had ever approached the job with as much enthusiasm as Jessica did, and here he was raining on her parade. He reached over and took her hand. "I'm sorry, Jess. What you've done is really great. But . . ."

"You're not used to hanging out at country

clubs where there's no action?" she suggested.

He grimaced. "It's not just that. It's other stuff." Nick rearranged the salt-and-pepper shakers, stalling. "Maybe this isn't the best time to have this conversation." He rubbed his hand over his face, wishing they didn't have to have it at all.

"What?" she pressed, leaning forward.

It wasn't going to be easy. But it wasn't going to be any easier tomorrow or the next day. "There's a reason I don't date policewomen," he said bluntly.

"Which is . . . ?"

"I like having professionals with me when I'm working. And I like having civilians around me when I'm not working. See? I like a little separation between my personal life and my professional life. Having you with me on this is making me feel . . ."

"Uh, *responsible?*"

"Yeah. Like I'm baby-sitting." He massaged his forehead with his thumb and forefinger, trying to make his perpetually tense facial muscles relax.

Jessica rested her elbows on the table, her blue-green eyes blazing with determination. "You don't have to be responsible for me."

"Yes, I do. You're not a cop," he reminded her. "You're a civilian."

"Don't you trust me?" she cried. "Look at what I've done. I've managed to disguise myself so thoroughly that Lila, Bruce, Tom, Dana, and all those snobs at the club have no idea it's me. Wouldn't you call that a pretty professional undercover operative?"

Nick's ears pricked up. Jessica had said a lot. But

what she *hadn't* said was far more revealing. He stuck a tongue into his cheek, reviewing the list she had run down for him before speaking. "What about Elizabeth?" he asked softly. "You didn't mention Elizabeth."

Jessica's cheeks flushed, and she dropped her eyes to the table, saying nothing. Now it was *her* turn to fiddle with the salt-and-pepper shakers.

Nick fought the urge to pound the table. "Elizabeth knows, doesn't she? When she followed you to the ladies' room, she knew who you were. Your cover is blown."

"She's my *sister*," Jessica protested. "Just because she recognized me doesn't mean anybody *else* did."

"Yeah. But your cover is blown, and *you didn't tell me!*" Nick hissed. His hands shook slightly. How could he convey to her how serious this was? "You don't make decisions affecting safety based on *might be, could be,* or *I'm having too much fun to stop,*" he told her angrily. "In a different situation a blunder like that could make the difference between living and dying."

Jessica's lips trembled. "I'm sorry," she said softly. "I just wanted to stay on this with you and—"

"Why can't you see that it's exactly that kind of childish *I want* behavior that makes it impossible for me to trust you in a police situation?" Nick slammed his newspaper down on the seat. It made a satisfyingly loud noise, and Jessica jumped. "I'm going to the men's room," he announced.

"But *Ni*-ick . . ."

He stood up and moved quickly through the diner, his stomach in nine kinds of knots. He felt as if

31

the top of his head was about to blow off. And he didn't answer her either. He didn't trust himself to speak—not if he wanted to keep dating her. And he did. He *did!* Jessica was beautiful. Bright and witty too. Plus, on top of it all, she was the most exciting woman he'd ever met. But she was also a loose cannon, and she could easily get somebody killed. Herself. Him. Some innocent bystander. You had to be able to trust a partner. Trust him or her to tell you anything and everything that might affect an investigation or safety. With this too-late revelation, he wasn't sure he could trust Jessica anymore.

The men's room was overly air-conditioned, but the blast of cold air felt good. He studied his face in the mirror over the sink. His cheeks and neck were flushed with temper. But he couldn't help smiling crookedly at his reflection.

If it wasn't for his signature leather jacket, his own mother wouldn't be able recognize him. Jessica had made some major changes in his appearance to make this undercover operation work. His shaggy brown hair had been cut and combed back. He wore glasses with wire frames, a polo shirt, and pressed khakis. She'd even doused him with some kind of upscale cologne. The makeover was pretty convincing. As far as Nick knew, nobody had made him. *Unless Elizabeth spotted me—which she probably did if she recognized Jessica,* he mused unhappily. *Elizabeth's sharp enough to put it together.*

Nick groaned out loud. Elizabeth had probably told Scott Sinclair. And Scott had probably told someone else. And so on, and so on . . .

Furiously Nick pulled a paper towel from the dispenser, held it under the cold water, and ran it over his forehead and cheeks until his irritation subsided. *Get a grip, Fox,* he told himself. *Chill out. Why are you getting so tense over this thing? It's nothing. It's stupid. There's no case. No danger. No reason to get this worked up.*

Nick tossed the towel in the wastebasket. It was time to wrap it up. Write a report. Throw it in the dead file and move on with his life with Jessica firmly filed under *G* for girlfriend and not *P* for partner.

He took a last look at himself in the mirror. The expression on his face told him he hadn't even managed to convince himself. "So, Nick?" he asked his reflection. "If it's a nowhere case, why *is* Elizabeth interested?"

Unfortunately his reflection didn't seem to have any answers. Nick took a comb from his back pocket and ran it through his hair, thinking.

"What's so important it's worth skipping classes to shop for it?" Isabella Ricci asked.

"Oh, please. Like *you've* never done it before," Lila replied with a laugh as she scanned the racks of Evita's, one of Sweet Valley's poshest boutiques. "Anyway, it's a reception this afternoon at the club for Paul Krandall's father. Paul's a Verona Springs VIP, you know, and Paul's dad is a congressman in Washington."

Denise Waters whistled. "I guess everybody will be turning out in their best VIP duds."

"Right," Lila said. "So it's megaimportant that I wear the right thing."

Lila was glad she had been able to convince two of her favorite Theta Alpha Theta sisters to come into town with her. Even though Lila had more money to spend on clothes than almost anybody else in their sorority, she didn't always trust her taste. Isabella was older and very sophisticated. Denise's taste was eccentric, but she was great at helping Lila assemble attention-getting outfits. Together they made a good consulting team. She had tried recruiting Jessica, her best friend, but for some reason no one had answered at the Wakefield twins' dorm room. Elizabeth was probably off in pursuit of actual learning while Jessica was snoring too loudly to hear the phone.

Lila removed a peach-colored, asymmetrical linen jacket and crumpled the sleeve in her hand. When she released the fabric, the creases didn't relax. It remained crisscrossed with wrinkles. Disgusted, she put it back on the rack. By the time she drove from campus to the country club, her seat belt would have rendered the jacket a complete mess. *Maybe I need a knit,* she thought.

"I saw Paul Krandall's picture in the paper," Denise said. "He's really cute. Is he dating anybody? Not that I have any personal interest or anything because as we *all* know, I'm *madly* in love with Winston Egbert."

Isabella giggled. "Which is sort of like saying you're madly in love with the Mad Hatter. Winston *is* wonderfully weird."

"And therefore perfect for me," Denise responded.

"But that doesn't mean I can't be curious. So? *Is* Paul dating anybody?" she pressed.

"Paul's engaged to Bunny Sterling," Lila answered.

"Who's Bunny Sterling?" Isabella asked.

"She's a VIP too," Lila answered shortly. "Her dad is a movie producer at CCR Studios. He produced *Island of the T-Rex Babes, Part Two*."

"Ugh! Winston and I saw that one," Denise cried.

Lila and Isabella looked at their friend in astonishment.

"Um . . . there wasn't anything else left at the video store," Denise insisted with a nervous giggle. "It was really, really bad."

"I'm sure it was," Lila remarked, feeling a little flicker of satisfaction. She wasn't too crazy about Bunny for a lot of reasons.

One: She had dated Bruce. OK, so it was only one date. But it didn't take a Sigmund Freud to figure out why Bruce felt so antagonistic toward Paul. He was *jealous*. Bruce couldn't possibly be interested in Bunny anymore, obviously, but it sure did bug him that she was engaged to somebody else.

Two: Bunny managed to work the fact that her dad was a movie producer into the conversation about fifty times every hour. It was *beyond* irritating.

Three: Being engaged to the VIP alpha dog had made Bunny insufferable. It was as if she thought that made her leaderette of the pack. The only VIP more powerful than Paul was Pepper Danforth.

Maybe Bunny should have tried to get engaged to her, Lila thought with a giggle.

Unfortunately Lila had to be nice to Bunny if she wanted to get in the VIP Circle. She was Paul's fiancée *and* Pepper's best friend. And the two of them were *very* influential. It was a high-society double whammy.

"It's *so* unfair," Lila murmured under her breath. As she whirled around in search of the perfect ensemble, Lila glanced out the window of the boutique and discovered none other than Paul Krandall standing on the curb near the newsstand. "Well, speak of the devil."

Isabella pointed out the window. "Isn't that him?"

"Yes," Lila said happily. "Come on. I'll introduce you." Lila took her friends by the arm and hustled them out of Evita's. "Paul! Yoo-hoo!"

Paul stood by the newsstand clad in a pullover knit shirt with khaki shorts and hiking boots, a newspaper under his arm. When he turned to meet her call, his eyebrows furrowed in apparent annoyance.

Lila stopped in her tracks. *Uh-oh,* she thought. *Did I gaffe?*

The annoyed look vanished in an instant, and Paul's face relaxed into its usual bland expression. Lila breathed a sigh of relief. He must have been frowning into the glare of the sun.

"Lila! Long time no see, old girl," Paul bellowed, laughing as if he had just said the funniest thing in the world.

Lila giggled politely. "Paul, I want you to meet my friends, Isabella Ricci and Denise Waters."

"How do you do?" Isabella said.

Paul held up a copy of *Scene* and pointed to his picture. He grinned broadly. "I do fine. That's me. See? With the trophy." Paul lifted the paper higher so that the photograph was level with his face. He struck a silly pose and cut his eyes toward the picture.

Lila giggled again. Paul threw back his head and howled like a hyena.

"I thought your dad was in town," Lila said when Paul settled down. "Aren't you spending the day with him?"

Paul seemed momentarily taken aback. "Oh yeah. I am. But . . ." He pointed to the stack of newspapers. "I wanted to get some extra copies of *Scene* for my friends," he answered.

"It's too bad Bunny's not in the picture," Denise said with a little smile. Her elbow nudged Lila's arm slightly.

"Bunny?" Paul repeated blankly.

"Uh . . . your *fiancée*?" Isabella offered.

"Oh, right. Of course," Paul said. "It's a long story—"

Suddenly a large cargo van came around the corner with a roar, and they all jumped back from the curb.

"Hey, drive much?" Denise hollered after the van.

Lila shot her a warning look.

"Whoops," Denise said meekly. "Pardon me."

Paul laughed and clapped. "Well, listen, I've got to get going. Busy, busy, busy," he said loftily before he ran across the street to get into a midsize sedan.

"Is that Paul's car?" Isabella asked, wrinkling her nose.

"No," Lila answered, still steaming at Denise for acting so coarsely in front of Paul. "He's got a Porsche. Maybe it's in the shop or something."

"Never mind that," Isabella said. "Don't you think it's weird that he didn't say anything about Bunny?"

"Maybe not." Denise held up a page of the *Scene* insert. "Look, here's a big article about CCR Studios. It says CCR's losing so much money on its recent flops that it may go out of business."

"Awww, poor Bunny," Lila said, her lips curving into a smile. If Bunny's dad's studio was sinking, then Bunny's lustre was probably fading fast. Stars in the VIP Circle glittered brightly, but not for long. Not when Lila Fowler was around to take the shine off them.

Chapter
Four

"Where are you from?" the smiling waitress asked as she removed Nick's empty plate of eggs and toast.

"Argentina," Jessica answered with a heavy accent. "A ranch just outside Buenos Aires. I am an exchange student at the University of Sweet Valley."

"I thought maybe you were a Myrna Ray makeup saleslady. You sure did give yourself a makeover. I was hoping you could give me a few beauty tips."

Jessica smiled. "Unfortunately I am not in the business of makeup. Coffee, that is where my fortune lies. My beauty tip is to go after the excitement in life. The . . . how do you say . . . gusto? Take the llama by the horns, that is my philosophy."

"That's good advice. Unfortunately we don't get a whole lot of excitement around *here*." The waitress chuckled as she wiped the table under the plate. After a few vigorous swipes she tucked the rag into the pocket of her orange polyester waitress uniform.

"I'll be back in a minute with more coffee. Maybe it's some your family grew."

The waitress walked away, leaving Jessica with nothing to do but tap her long, bloodred nails on the Formica and wait for Nick to return from his snit. Why was it so hard for him to get it? He didn't seem to understand that a big part of his appeal to her was his job. The chance to participate in his life. A life that was grown up, real, and on the edge.

Jessica could have her pick of college boys. They were all cute and charming. And they were all crazy about her. But she was tired of that life. She needed a man who offered excitement and an opportunity to grow. A man who, as Lila would say, could help her achieve her goal.

The waitress reappeared, holding two coffeepots, one with an orange rim, one with a green rim. "More coffee?"

"Yes, thank you," Jessica answered absently. "Decaf for me. Regular for him."

The waitress lifted her eyebrows in surprise, and Jessica mentally kicked herself. She'd forgotten to use her accent! "Decaf is corrrrect? *¿Sí?*" she added quickly.

The waitress's look of surprise vanished. *"Sí,"* she answered cheerfully. "Your English is excellent!"

"Gracias," Jessica said, glad Nick had been in the men's room. All it would take was one more goof and he'd read it as proof positive that she wasn't cut out for undercover police work.

She turned her head and looked through the window at the parking lot. The diner was on the outskirts of town and well off the beaten path. She knew she still needed to watch her step. But staying in character was so *hard*. She'd made a lot of mistakes—none she'd ever admit to, of course.

Maybe Nick's right, she thought unhappily. *Maybe I'm not cut out for undercover police work. A real undercover policewoman would never have blown her cover like that.*

On the other hand, a real undercover policewoman would have been *trained*. Taught how to get in character and stay in character. She didn't have experience, just instinct. And instinct had been good enough—so far.

As Jessica stirred her coffee the roar of an engine drew her attention back toward the window. A large cargo van pulled in off the highway and idled in the parking lot. Then someone stepped out of a parked sedan in the corner of the lot and approached the red cab of the van. Jessica squinted. It was Paul Krandall!

Paul walked from the car to the truck with his head swiveling almost imperceptibly left and right. If Jessica hadn't been taught that same reconnaissance technique, she wouldn't even have noticed what he was doing—which was taking an inventory of who might be watching. *Why does he care?* she wondered.

He and the driver of the van exchanged a few words before the driver got out and Paul got in. Jessica watched, stunned, as Paul backed the van onto the highway and drove off. The van driver got into the car Paul had been driving, pulled onto the highway, and headed the opposite way.

How weird! Jessica thought, gnawing on her heavily made-up lower lip. *How incredibly weird!* She strained to read the van's plates, but it was already too far away.

41

Maybe if she ran outside, she could get a good look.

Just as she was getting out of the booth Nick came out of the men's room. He hurried over and put his hand on her shoulder. "Please don't leave. I want to talk to you," Nick said quietly. "I wasn't fair, and—"

"Never mind about that," Jessica responded, shaking off his hand. "Wait here. I'll be back."

"Jes—uh, Perdita! Where are you going? *Perdita!*"

Jessica didn't wait to explain. She bolted out of the diner and across the parking lot to the edge of the highway. The vehicle was still visible down the long, shimmering highway. Too far to read the plates, though. "Darn!" Jessica murmured. "Chrome cab, red van, missing mud flap," she recited, trying to commit to memory the information she *had* been able to gather. She trotted back into the diner, giggling when she noticed Nick watching her through the window, a quizzical expression on his face.

"What was that all about?" he asked when she returned.

"I'm not sure. But here's what I just saw." Quickly Jessica described the short scene she had just witnessed.

She sat back proudly waiting for Nick to react. Instead he shrugged as if he had little or no interest. "Anything unusual about the van?" he asked.

"Just the missing mud flap," she answered.

Nick shrugged again. "Paul Krandall's dad is a congressman. He's coming through town on a campaign stop. It's probably a van full of Vote for Krandall stuff."

Jessica could almost hear the air leaking out of her balloon. She felt her face fall.

He leaned forward. "Hey! Come on. Don't look like that. Your instincts are great. You've got your eyes open, and you're asking questions. That's what policing's all about. But it's also about being *logical.* Quit worrying about what's in the van. Concentrate on what you know. You know Elizabeth's working on something. Find out what it is. Get her to tell you."

"I can't. . . ."

"Yes, you can."

"Elizabeth won't tell me anything," she insisted.

"Lean," Nick said with gentle emphasis. "You want to help me out? Find out what your sister knows. You got a moral problem? Ask yourself this: Why doesn't a reporter think helping the police is more important than getting a story? Why don't reporters care about justice?"

"Elizabeth cares about justice!" Jessica cried. "She cares more about justice than anybody I know."

"Even more than me?"

"Maybe."

Nick smiled. "Then why won't she help?"

Jessica sighed. "I don't know. Because she's competitive. And Tom Watts is on the story too. Tom totally broke her heart. Maybe that's warped her judgment or something. *But* I think I know a way to get her to cooperate," she said, an idea beginning to form. She leaned forward, determined to extract a promise. "If I find out anything, can we stay on this? Together?"

Nick nodded. "If you find out anything that justifies further investigation. Sure."

"Promise?"

"I promise. But if you don't find anything, the case is closed. Deal?" He extended his hand.

Jessica reached across the table. "Deal," she agreed, giving his hand a firm shake.

"Now, no tricks," he cautioned.

Jessica giggled mischievously. "Well, not on *you*."

"Let's go back over what we know," Scott suggested as he headed the car toward the Sweet Valley County records office.

Elizabeth pulled down the passenger side sun visor so she could read through her story notes. "We know that not long ago, Dwayne Mendoza, a caddy at Verona Springs, was found dead, probably murdered. Another caddy, Brandon Phillips, is being held by the police, possibly charged. Juan Mendoza, Dwayne's uncle, disappeared from the club after warning us about people 'getting away with murder.'"

"What do you think that means?" Scott asked.

"I bet that means the real suspect is still at large," Elizabeth said decisively. "Also missing is Manuel Coimbra, a busboy at the club. He disappeared around the time of Mendoza's death. Mail continues to be sent to him in care of the club. Nothing of much importance, except the postcard notifying him that his voting location has been changed."

"Which makes no sense because he was a resident alien and therefore not entitled to vote," Scott said.

"Right."

"Plus his name was spelled wrong on the card— with an *o* instead of a *u*."

Elizabeth nodded. "Maybe it was sent to the wrong guy?"

"Probably just a typo. Nobody spells Manuel with an *o*." Scott shifted gears as they made a sharp turn. "So how does Paul Krandall fit in?" he mused. "Why did he lie about the money? He said he won it from Bruce Patman. Where did the wad of cash come from if Bruce Patman gave him a check, like you told me?"

Elizabeth chewed the end of her pen. "Maybe the cash isn't related to the murder at all. Maybe Paul's got a hustling scam going, and Bruce wasn't the only victim. Maybe he'd been plucking pigeons for a few days. Maybe we've got two stories instead of one."

Scott tilted back his head, reached up, and absently scratched the underside of his chin. His nails made a faint scraping sound against his stubble.

Involuntarily Elizabeth caught her breath. The gesture reminded her vividly of Tom. The tilt of the head. The set of the lips. The intimate, masculine sound.

She closed her eyes as a wave of longing washed over her. No one had ever made her feel the way Tom Watts had. No one had ever kissed her the way Tom had. Whenever she'd seen him kissing Dana— which seemed to happen an awful lot—she'd felt as if her heart might break.

Elizabeth sighed. How she wished his lips would touch hers again, just once. They almost had the day before, when they were on the verge of sharing their information with each other in the club's parking lot. His head had bowed so close to hers, their lips just about to—

"Hello?" Scott jostled her arm.

She came reluctantly back to the present. Just as he had in the parking lot yesterday, Scott interrupted her right when her fantasies were becoming realized. "What?" she asked, trying to hide the irritation in her voice.

"Paul and the money. What's the deal?"

"Tom . . . Tom was in the parking lot when the police came. I could tell by the expression on his face that the money was significant somehow. He knows something we don't."

"And we know a few things he doesn't," Scott answered. "Any chance he might want to trade information?"

Elizabeth dropped her gaze to her lap. "I tried that, remember? No dice, thanks to you."

Scott fiddled with his collar in obvious discomfort. "So . . . uh . . . we just have to proceed with what *we* know, which is that a busboy named Manuel Coimbra disappeared around the same time as the murder. And that Paul Krandall lied about where he got the money in his pocket."

Elizabeth shot a look at Scott out of the corner of her eye. Was she imagining things, or did he look dissatisfied? Elizabeth had a reputation for being a crack investigative reporter. Was he thinking she wasn't living up to her rep? She started to say something, then changed her mind. If he had any criticisms, she really didn't want to hear them right now. She was feeling too insecure, too vulnerable.

Scott exited the freeway and pulled into the parking

46

lot of the old-fashioned county records office. It was an imposing white stone building with a white cupola. Wide marble steps led to heavy brass-and-glass double doors. Together they got out of Scott's car and hurried across the lot toward the steps in silence. When they approached the doors, Scott reached over her shoulder to push open the door for her.

Elizabeth felt her heart flutter again. Another Tom gesture.

Forget Tom, she told herself sternly. *Tom's through with you. How much clearer does he have to make it?* She felt a gentle hand on her arm and jumped, her heart leaping into her throat.

Scott laughed. "Did I startle you?"

Elizabeth shook her head. "No. I . . . I'm just ticklish there," she lied. For one brief second she'd wondered if her yearning for Tom had somehow managed to conjure him up in the flesh. Tom had taken her arm in exactly that way a thousand times. *Never again,* she thought unhappily as Scott guided her inside.

The county records office was obviously not the busiest place on a Wednesday morning. They only had to wait on line for a few minutes before it was their turn to be helped.

"I'm looking for information on this man." Elizabeth handed a slip of paper with the name Manuel Coimbra written on it to the woman behind the desk. "He's moved, and I'm trying to find an updated address."

The clerk took the piece of paper and asked them to have a seat in the waiting area. Elizabeth and Scott sat

47

down in the molded plastic chairs that lined the perimeter of the room and waited. And waited. And *waited*.

Elizabeth jumped up and approached the counter. "Excuse me?"

"Yes?" the clerk answered.

"I'm sorry, but . . . what's taking so long?"

"I'm having trouble locating a Manuel Coimbra. Are you sure you have the correct spelling?"

"Yes! Wait—I mean . . . try it with an *o*," she corrected, her cheeks reddening. *"M-a-n-o-e-l."*

The clerk raised her eyebrows and went back to work while Elizabeth dragged herself back to her chair. And still waited. Even though she might have gotten the name right this time, it hadn't made things happen any more quickly.

A large clock on the wall made Elizabeth keenly aware that precious time was passing. As the minutes ticked by she watched for some expression of irritation or impatience from Scott. But he sat quietly beside her with his arms folded, perfectly calm. He didn't even jiggle his foot. She couldn't help thinking that in the same situation, Tom Watts would have been bouncing off the walls, and she would have to have been his calming influence. Now *she* was the one who felt like jumping out of her skin.

"Ms. Wakefield?"

"Here!" Elizabeth practically shouted. She leaped from her seat and hurried toward the counter, where the clerk held a computer printout.

"I was able to locate a Manoel Coimbra," the clerk announced. "With an *o*."

"And?" Elizabeth asked excitedly.

"I'm very sorry, but this man is no longer living."

Elizabeth's heart banged against her rib cage. She heard Scott sharply draw in his breath. *Another murder!* her mind shouted in a panic. She felt her lip tremble. *I bet the gardener who tried to warn us is dead too!*

She'd always thought of herself as a top-notch reporter. How could she have been so arrogant? People were getting *killed*. And it was all her fault—because she'd been more concerned with beating Tom to the story than behaving like a responsible journalist. She had moved too fast and too clumsily. Asked too many questions and aroused suspicions. She was so ashamed and heartsick, she could hardly speak.

Defeated, she took the computer printout from the clerk's hand and read it. Scott leaned against her arm, reading along with her.

He gasped and snatched it from her hand. "Hold it, Elizabeth. He died in 1991? That was *years* ago."

Relief washed over Elizabeth's body. *Then it can't be my fault,* she thought thankfully. "But how—"

"Thank you," Scott said to the clerk. He took Elizabeth's arm and steered her out of the office. "Let's go upstairs to the newspaper archives and look up obituaries," he whispered. "See if we can make any sense out of this—in private."

"OK."

He and Elizabeth hurried up to the second-floor archives, where several carrels were equipped with computer terminals. Elizabeth threw herself into a chair and dropped her backpack on the floor. Scott pulled up a chair and sat at her elbow.

Elizabeth clicked the mouse on the obituary icon and then typed in the year. After a brief delay the computer asked her to type in the name. With quick keystrokes she typed Manoel Coimbra. Holding her breath, she waited, praying the data bank was up-to-date. She could feel Scott's even breathing on her neck.

The computer made a blip sound, and Elizabeth's eyes widened. "There it is. Manoel Coimbra's obit." Her heartbeat doubled as she read. "Look. It says he was *not* a resident alien."

"Where was he from?" Scott asked. He read aloud as the screen scrolled. "He was a naturalized U.S. citizen from Brazil. . . . Arrived in the U.S. in 1970 . . . worked as a plant foreman until retiring in 1990 . . . and died in 1991 of a heart attack. *At age seventy-six!*"

"Not exactly a teenager," Elizabeth commented with a shaky laugh.

"It's got to be a mistake," Scott muttered. "I'm going back downstairs."

Elizabeth caught at his sleeve. "Not so fast."

Scott looped a stray lock of hair behind his ear. "It's the wrong guy. It has to be."

"Maybe not. Look where he lived. The zip code. That would put him in the same voting district."

Scott's brow furrowed. "You're right. But what does it mean?"

"Let's go outside," Elizabeth said. "I need to think."

Once outside, Elizabeth sat on the top step and turned the facts over and over in her head. No matter how she rearranged the pieces of the puzzle, she still couldn't get a clear picture. It was there. She could almost see it in her mind's eye. But it was fuzzy.

Upset and frustrated, Elizabeth let out a little groan of impatience and crumpled the computer page in her hand.

"Hey, hey, hey!" Scott soothed. "Stay cool."

Elizabeth removed her baseball cap and wiped her sweating forehead with the sleeve of her sweatshirt. "I'm trying. But it's so frustrating. I feel like I'm this close, but . . ." She grimaced. "Maybe I spent too much time working in television news. My brain's gone stale. I feel like I'm letting you down," she added softly. "Letting the paper down. The whole medium of print journalism down! I probably should stick to puff pieces."

Scott let out a groan of protest. "No way!" He shook her arm. "You're not letting me down. Believe me. I'm totally impressed with the way you're moving on this."

"I'm moving with the speed of a glacier."

Scott chuckled good-naturedly. "You *have* been in TV too long," he agreed. "But it hasn't made you a bad investigative reporter. It's made you *impatient*. You can't wrap up every story in time for the six o'clock news. If you try, you jump to conclusions— the *wrong* conclusions. Lighten up and be realistic."

Elizabeth breathed deeply. Scott was right. She wasn't racing to meet a deadline. She was trying to get to the truth. *But I'm going to beat Tom Watts to it if I can,* she thought grimly. *I almost lost my nerve*

51

up there, but from now on it's full steam ahead.

Scott put his hand on her arm and squeezed. "Elizabeth, I've got something I need to talk to you about, and . . ."

Elizabeth gulped, her stomach tightening. Scott was a friend, but he was pushing hard to be more than a friend. Elizabeth was nowhere near ready for a new relationship. She gently, but firmly, moved her arm.

Scott smiled tightly, opened his hands as if to say "sorry," and cleared his throat. Elizabeth's cheeks burned slightly with embarrassment.

"I wasn't sure how you'd feel," he began. "So I decided not to say anything until I was absolutely sure. But I think you're going to be able to see Brandon Phillips today."

Elizabeth's embarrassment was immediately forgotten. "You're kidding! Today?" she asked, torn between resentment and admiration. "Why didn't you tell me? I'm hardly even prepared!"

He shrugged. "I didn't want to get your hopes up. But now I think you need all the hope-getting-up you can get."

"Wow . . . maybe I can finally start coming up with some answers," Elizabeth said. "How did you swing this, Scott?"

"Smooth talk. The same way I swing everything." He smiled. "I'll call and make sure we can do it this afternoon. Then after that we can zip out to the country club in time for the Krandall reception."

"Do you think we really need to go?" Elizabeth asked.

"It's hard to know," Scott answered. "But as members of the student media, we should probably be there. It might look suspicious if we're not, you know?"

"You're right. Besides, my puff piece wouldn't be complete without mentioning a visiting VIP in the VIP Circle," she finished with a laugh.

Scott playfully pushed the bill of her cap down. "You're going to write the hardest-hitting puff piece this town has ever seen. Come on. Let's get back to campus and change." He stood and pulled her to her feet. "I think it's important for the paper's image that we look as professional as possible. Do you have a suit? Navy blue? Gray? Something like that?"

"I've got a black blazer and a gray skirt," she answered. "It's pretty boring. Maybe I should wear something that looks dressier."

"No, no. Wear the black blazer and gray skirt. We want to look very conservative and businesslike. It gives us credibility. We don't want to look like college kids."

He draped his arm over her shoulders, and Elizabeth fought the impulse to recoil. Why did he keep touching her? Especially when she sent him such clear *don't touch* signals?

It's just his style, she told herself. *Some guys touch.*

Still, she wished he wouldn't.

Chapter Five

"Please, hallway, stay empty," Jessica whispered as she crept along the Dickenson Hall second-floor hallway with her high-heeled shoes in hand. Several doors were open to catch the cross breeze created by the windows, and Jessica didn't want any of the occupants to hear her footsteps and look to see who was in the hall. They might wonder why a glamorous Argentinean heiress was letting herself into Jessica and Elizabeth Wakefield's room.

When she reached the door of room 28, she listened closely for signs that someone was about to burst out of one of the dorm rooms. But all was quiet on the Dickenson front. She heard no conversation or laughter. Just the strains of classical music that usually indicated serious studying.

Safely inside, the room was quiet and hushed. No Elizabeth anywhere. Jessica caught a glimpse of herself in the mirror and gasped, feeling as if she had surprised an intruder in her room. With her dark hair, heavy eyebrows, and extreme lipstick, she looked like a stranger even to herself. She felt like a stranger too, as if she were seeing the room for the first time and through different eyes.

Her own bed was littered with clothing, magazines, and stuffed animals. They were her things, but she couldn't summon up a feeling of ownership. They seemed like unimportant remnants of a former life.

The life of Jessica Wakefield, student.

Now she was Jessica Wakefield, undercover cop. A different person.

Elizabeth's side of the room was frighteningly orderly as usual. Her clothing was put away in the closet. Magazines were nowhere to be seen. Her stuffed animals were stashed away, along with all her textbooks, in a bookcase. A *bookcase!* Jessica didn't even know where her textbooks *were!* Disgustingly neat little piles of notebooks and papers were arranged on Elizabeth's desktop, reminding Jessica that she wasn't even sure where her *own* desk was underneath the mess.

Jessica looked at Elizabeth's desk cautiously. She had been crashing at Nick's for the last couple of days. Would Elizabeth think it was safe to leave her notes out in the open? Smiling slyly, she put her shoes on the floor, tiptoed toward the desk, and opened one of the notebooks. Elizabeth's neat handwriting listed the economic and political events precipitating the War of 1812.

"Oooh, stop the presses." Jessica flipped through

the rest of the pages, then pushed it aside. She opened the second notebook. Nothing but squiggly math problems. She picked up the third notebook and fanned the pages. More squiggly math problems.

Frustrated, she began rifling through the shelf above the desk, removing book after book and throwing them aside in frustration.

"*What* are you *doing*?"

Jessica let out a little screech and whirled around to see Elizabeth standing in the doorway, her eyes blazing like a two–hundred–alarm fire.

"I was—"

Elizabeth strode forward, snatched a notebook from Jessica's hand, and shoved it angrily back onto the shelf. "I can't believe this," she growled. Quickly and efficiently she restored order to the chaos Jessica had created.

Jessica's face burned scarlet with shame. "I'm sorry."

"Sorry doesn't cut it," Elizabeth snapped. "I can't believe you're actually snooping through my things. Trying to find my story notes, I bet. That's despicable."

Jessica's shame turned to outrage. She was prepared to apologize to her sister, but not to a story-hungry reporter. "No," she said. "What's despicable is holding up a police investigation because *you* want to keep your story to *yourself*."

Elizabeth flinched slightly. Her mouth tightened, and she stubbornly refused to meet Jessica's eyes.

"How can you let a murderer walk around loose just because you're mad at an old boyfriend?" she added, putting the icing on the cake.

Elizabeth dropped a book and glared ferociously at Jessica. "Don't judge me by your standards. That's the kind of thing *you* would do. Not me."

"Prove it."

Elizabeth turned away, neatening the shelves.

Jessica felt the edges of her lips curl up in a smile. She was getting to Elizabeth. She could tell. She'd argued with Elizabeth enough times to know that when Elizabeth didn't have an immediate comeback, she was in a major moral fix.

"If this were about finding the truth, you wouldn't care who got credit for cracking the story." Jessica crossed her arms confidently and leveled both barrels, ready to hit her sister where she lived. "You know, I think Nick may be right about women. Nick says women don't make good decisions. They let their emotions cloud their judgment. Kinda wacky, eh?" Sure, it was all a lie—Nick would never *really* say anything like that. But boy, it was the *right* lie.

Elizabeth's high-pitched scream of outrage let Jessica know she'd hit pay dirt. "Th-That's ridiculous!" she sputtered.

"Maybe so," Jessica challenged. "But the least you could do is behave as professionally as *Tom* is."

Elizabeth's eyes narrowed. "Are you saying that *Tom* is cooperating?"

He wasn't, of course, but that was exactly what Jessica wanted Elizabeth to think. She worked hard to keep from smirking at her own cleverness.

Elizabeth slammed the drawer of her desk shut and leaned back against it, raking a few loose strands of hair back off her forehead with her fingers. Her chest heaved angrily.

Jessica watched Elizabeth closely, holding her breath. Elizabeth had taken the bait. She was about to fall right into Jessica's hands. Tell her everything she knew. *Nick will be so proud of me,* she thought happily.

"Well," Elizabeth responded after a long, thoughtful pause, "if you've got Tom's cooperation, you don't need *mine,* do you?"

Jessica groaned. She'd miscalculated again!

The phone rang, and Elizabeth reached for it. "Hello?" She eyed Jessica warily, then turned her back and spoke in a low tone so she couldn't be overheard.

Jessica went to her closet and pretended to busy herself with searching for a pair of shoes. She couldn't remember the last time she had *put* a pair of shoes in her closet, but it was the right cover for listening in on Elizabeth's conversation.

"This afternoon? . . . Now? . . . That doesn't give me much time to prepare. What about the reception? . . . OK . . . OK . . . I'll meet you out front."

Elizabeth hung up the phone and practically lunged past Jessica toward her own closet. She yanked a black blazer and gray skirt out of the closet. "I can't argue with you anymore. I've got to change and get out of here."

"Where are you going?" Jessica asked, hoping she sounded as if it didn't really matter to her one way or the other.

Elizabeth glared at her. "No comment," she

replied. "And stay out of my stuff. There's nothing there that can help you anyway."

The Verona Springs Country Club was coming to life when Tom got there. The gravel-covered parking lot was about half full. Tom figured it would really fill up when the reception started.

Tom decided to review the layout one more time. It never hurt to know where to zig and how to zag when the game heated up. The ballroom was at the far end of the club. It had glass doors that led to the patio and pool area. It also had a back door that opened onto a breezeway connecting to the kitchen. Waiters and staff used that door to enter and leave the facility with trays and pitchers to avoid colliding with guests coming in and out the patio door. Across from the breezeway there was another door marked Employees Only that led up to the employees' lounge on the second floor.

Tom skirted the front entrance and entered the club through the outdoor patio area. The tables were filling up with lunchtime guests, and the air was full of the soft plopping sounds of tennis balls.

He didn't see Dana around anywhere. She was probably off with the quartet, going over the music. He spotted Pepper and Anderson, but no Bunny or Paul. No Elizabeth or Scott either.

Tom chewed his lip, at a loss. He had no idea where to go from here on this story. He decided to head up to the employees' lounge.

But when he got upstairs and pushed open the

door, the lounge was empty. Nobody sat on the long canvas sofas or around the glass-top tables, where the staff ate their lunch.

Tom walked over to the large window that overlooked the patio and the grounds. From this angle he could see almost the entire club. The shimmering sun hovered in the cloudless blue sky above the mountains. It was a gorgeous day. One of those California afternoons that made lonesome people lonesome enough to cry.

Attractive young couples walked up and down the gravel paths between the tennis courts. A girl with long blond hair tightened her ponytail as she stood laughing with her boyfriend. The gesture reminded him so much of Elizabeth, his chest tightened.

He missed her. Missed being part of a couple. Missed being with somebody who knew what he was thinking before he knew it himself.

"You're here early?"

He turned to see Dana in the doorway, a soda in her hand. Her tight zebra print jeans looked painted on, and a black long-sleeve jersey showed off her bare shoulders and her hand-drawn heart.

"I thought I'd get here a little early and see if you needed any moral support," he lied, wondering how she could get away with wearing something like that to a string quartet performance for a congressman—especially when she was a quarter of the quartet.

She smiled slyly, as if she suspected he was shmoozing her.

Well, I am, he told himself. *Maybe Elizabeth isn't*

the only woman capable of reading my thoughts.

"Thanks," Dana cooed, moving across the room to stand beside him at the window. Strands of her long curly hair tickled his cheeks, and he could smell her citrusy perfume. But it didn't make any difference.

Here, right next to him, was a woman who could easily give any guy what he wanted. She was bright, talented, ambitious, sexy, and beautiful. Mind-bendingly beautiful. There might have been a time when she could have given Tom everything he wanted too. But that was before he fell in love with Elizabeth Wakefield. And now, while this beautiful woman planted gentle kisses on his neck, Tom couldn't help but feel totally and completely alone.

A burst of longing exploded in Tom's chest, and for a moment he thought he might actually burst into tears. The idea of feeling this lonely and miserable for the rest of his life was almost unbearable. He blinked back the tears and swallowed the lump in his throat.

"I'm going to have to split in a couple of minutes," Dana murmured, apparently unaware that Tom was fighting tears. "The quartet's got to go over some arrangements before the reception. Can you hang out on your own?"

"Oh, sure," Tom replied, struggling to keep his voice steady. "If I get bored, I'll . . . I'll take a walk around and see what Bun and Pep are up to."

Dana giggled and rubbed up against him. "OK, then. I'll see you later."

Tom lingered at the window after she left. The golf course stretched out and disappeared over the rise of the hill like an emerald green carpet. It was hard to believe anything sinister could have taken place on the manicured grounds of Verona Springs.

But something had. Where was the gardener who had tipped him and Elizabeth off in the first place? On the run? Dead? A shiver ran up Tom's spine, reminding him that there was more at stake here than getting back *at*—or getting back *with*—Elizabeth Wakefield.

The pro in the caddy shack had told Tom the old man had retired. Under the circumstances it seemed improbable. Who was lying? The pro? *Maybe he honestly thought the old man had retired,* Tom thought. *Which would mean that somebody in management is lying.*

The door swung open, making Tom jump.

"Hola!" Carlos, the young headwaiter, walked in. His voice was friendly but held a note of curiosity.

"Hi," Tom said. "I was here with Dana. She's in the quartet."

"Of course." Carlos continued to smile but said nothing more.

"The quartet that plays at tea," Tom continued, feeling somewhat uncomfortable under Carlos's questioning gaze. "They're going to play at a reception this afternoon for Congressman Krandall. She just left to go rehearse, but . . . well, I can't help but linger behind and enjoy this view."

"I see."

Tom couldn't tell if Carlos resented Tom's presence in the lounge or not. "If I'm in the way—"

"No, no," Carlos said quickly. He lifted his hands and opened them to indicate that Tom was welcome.

"It's a nice place to wait. A nice place to sit and think, or talk." He walked over to where Tom stood and looked out, admiring the view. "It is a pleasure to work in such a beautiful place. A privilege."

There was a long pause.

Outside, on one of the many tennis courts, Tom watched Paul Krandall volley with Bunny. Carlos's eyes narrowed, and his lips tightened as his gaze came to rest on Paul. What did Carlos's expression mean?

Was he angry at Paul?

Afraid of Paul?

Tom felt even more certain now that the cash Paul had was the money Carlos collected from the other Hispanic workers. And he had a pretty fair idea how he had gotten it. It was very possible that they didn't have the right papers and Paul was blackmailing them, forcing Carlos to be the bagman.

"It is probably hard for someone like you to imagine what it is like to be desperate for work," Carlos said softly.

Tom started to argue that he *could* imagine—that he was sensitive enough to imagine the plight of people less fortunate than himself. But he sensed Carlos stiffen.

Tom closed his mouth with a snap. Carlos was right. He couldn't imagine what it was like. Not really. Whatever he might "imagine" would simply underline the fact that he was incredibly ignorant of the harsh reality of true poverty—especially when paired with discrimination.

When Tom's family had been killed in an auto

accident, he began to realize that the experience set him apart from the rest of the world. No one who hadn't been through it themselves could ever begin to imagine the scope of the tragedy or the depth of his pain. It would have irritated him for someone to trivialize that experience by claiming the ability to "imagine" it.

Tom was attending one of the finest colleges in the country. And he was an honor student. He might not get exactly the job he wanted. He might not get paid as much as he hoped. But there was no doubt at all that he could get a job. "No," he agreed softly. "I can't imagine what that's like. It must be very difficult."

Carlos said nothing for a long time. Then he nodded as if Tom had given him an answer he could respect. The two young men were silent as they watched the tennis game through the window. But Carlos's eyes didn't move back and forth with the ball. They remained focused on Paul.

What would happen, Tom wondered, *if I just came right out and asked Carlos how Paul had gotten the money—or if Paul was blackmailing him?* Tom decided to hold back. He needed information, but he didn't want to push Carlos too hard. He didn't want Carlos to disappear like the gardener had.

"The people who work here, the ones from Mexico and farther south, they are very grateful for the opportunity," Carlos continued, nodding toward a group of young busboys setting up tables on the patio.

"Gratitude sometimes makes people . . . ummm . . . *vulnerable,*" Tom suggested.

Carlos considered the remark. "Yes," he said quietly. "You're right."

Tom held his breath, hoping Carlos would elaborate. When he didn't, Tom took a chance. "They may not be as vulnerable as they think. Someone might have information that would help to protect them. Protect them from people who might *exploit* them."

Carlos snapped his head around. His dark eyes bored into Tom's, as if he were trying to decide how far to trust him.

Then the door opened again, and Carlos's face immediately closed up. His eyelids fell, shielding his dark, expressive eyes. A round, middle-aged man in a business suit stood in the doorway. "Carlos," he said pleasantly. "You'd better start setting up the ballroom for the Krandall reception."

"Yes, sir," Carlos answered respectfully. His gaze held Tom's for a second, and Tom wished he had a fraction of Elizabeth's intuition. What was Carlos trying to tell him?

Carlos left the employees' lounge, and the other man scrutinized Tom. "I'm Bill Phelps, the club manager. I don't think I know you," he said. "Are you one of the new caddies?"

Tom offered his hand. "No, sir. I'm a friend of Dana Upshaw's. She's one of the musicians. My name is Tom Watts. I'm also the news anchor for WSVU, the college television station. I'm covering the reception."

Mr. Phelps pumped Tom's hand enthusiastically. "Excellent. Excellent. I'm sure the congressman will be pleased. I never met a politician yet who didn't love media coverage. If you need anything at all, let me know. Or ask Carlos. Carlos will be able to help you."

Tom smiled. "Thank you."

Mr. Phelps beamed again and bustled out of the lounge. Tom sat down and wearily wondered if his radar was on the blink. Mr. Phelps hadn't seemed the least bit rattled that the campus press was on the scene—which would indicate that he had nothing to hide. The only blip on his radar screen was Paul Krandall. But how did Paul connect to the murdered caddy?

Carlos will be able to help you. Mr. Phelps's words echoed in Tom's brain.

"If only he would," he muttered in response.

Chapter Six

"Elizabeth, calm down," Scott begged.

"I can't calm down. I'm too angry. I can't believe Tom is actually insinuating himself into a police investigation. You know why he's doing it, don't you? So he can get to *me*. Find out what *I* know. Well, he can just forget it."

Scott took one hand off the wheel and put it over Elizabeth's. "Put it out of your mind," he urged. "You need to focus on this interview. I don't know if we'll be able to talk to this guy more than once. This may be your only chance to find out what we want to know. Don't blow it because of Tom Watts."

"You're right," Elizabeth agreed. She took some deep breaths. If Tom was at the reception, which she felt sure he would be, she could vent her anger then.

Elizabeth stared down at her black pumps. She and Scott were going to be the most conservatively dressed people at the reception. Scott was even wearing a suit. It was odd how he had insisted on it. California country club attire tended toward bright, colorful silks for women and blazers and slacks for men. She and Scott looked like they were on their way to work at the bank.

Scott pulled into the crowded parking lot of the Sweet Valley Prison. "Business must be good," he joked as they made the dispirited and depressing walk to the entrance. When the doors opened, they stepped off and stopped at a security desk.

"I'm Scott Sinclair. This is Elizabeth Wakefield. We have clearance to see Brandon Phillips," he said.

The blue-uniformed policewoman never changed expression. "Purse," she said curtly to Elizabeth.

Elizabeth put her purse on the desk. The policewoman glanced through it, then put it on a conveyor belt so it could pass through an x-ray machine. The policewoman nodded toward an electronic archway, instructing Elizabeth and Scott to walk through it. Scott set off a series of beeps immediately.

Two policemen started toward him, their hands held up, warning him not to proceed further. Scott backed up. One of the officers reached for a scanning device and waved it up and down the length of his body, then patted him down. Once Scott had surrendered his wallet, keys, nail clipper, change, and money clip, he was allowed to walk through the metal detector again. This time it made no noise.

After what seemed like an eternity, Scott and Elizabeth were finally escorted down a long hallway to a glassed-in conference room. Through the smudged glass of the window Elizabeth saw a small, forlorn-looking guy wearing an orange jumpsuit. His short blond hair looked dirty, and his complexion was pale and waxy with red blemishes.

His neatly folded hands rested on the table in front of him, and Elizabeth noticed with a shock that he was wearing handcuffs.

Well, what did you expect? she scolded herself. *He's a murderer—or at least the cops think he is.*

"You have half an hour." The guard whisked a magnetic card through a lock. Elizabeth and Scott stepped inside, and the guard closed the door behind them. An electronic ratcheting noise announced that they were locked in. Prisoners, just like Brandon Phillips.

"You guys look too young to be attorneys," Brandon commented.

"We're not attorneys," Elizabeth said, startled. "What made you think we were?"

Brandon leaned forward, visibly intent and upset. "I was told two attorneys wanted to talk to me. *That's* what made me think you were attorneys."

Stunned, Elizabeth looked to Scott for an explanation. Who would have told him they were attorneys?

Scott smiled wryly. "I never actually *said* we were attorneys," he said in a hedging tone.

Elizabeth was so flabbergasted, she could hardly speak. Scott had *lied* to get them this interview! *Lied* to prison officials!

Brandon's eyes narrowed suspiciously. "If you're not attorneys, what are you doing here?"

Scott unbuttoned his suit jacket and loosened his

tie. "Look. I'm sorry if we misled you, but—"

"I'll say you misled me," Brandon said angrily. "I thought you guys were here to give me some legal aid. Who are you?"

"Reporters," Scott answered.

Brandon rolled his eyes and slumped in his chair. "Oh, great!" he groaned. "Reporters. Just what I need. No reporter has helped me yet."

Elizabeth caught her breath, her outrage over Scott's misstep disappearing. Had Tom been here already? "What other reporters have you talked to? Anybody named *Tom Watts?*"

Brandon glared at her with loathing. "I haven't talked to any reporters because it's a waste of time and a waste of breath. But just for the record, I'll tell you what I told the cops. I didn't do it, and I don't have any story to tell unless you want to print the truth. And the truth is that *I am innocent. Clear enough?*" he shouted angrily.

Elizabeth fought the impulse to clutch at Scott's sleeve. Brandon Phillips seemed to be telling the truth. But he looked pretty murderously angry right now. Elizabeth didn't blame him. She felt pretty murderously angry herself.

Now that she knew Tom hadn't scooped her, she was free to turn her anger and outrage back on Scott. How dare Scott manipulate Brandon into talking to them? How dare he implicate her in a lie? They could get into real trouble for this. Trouble that would follow her into her professional career. "Scott—"

Scott took her arm and walked her to the side of

the room. "You can yell at me all day long when this is over," he whispered. "But right now you need to take advantage of this opportunity. OK?"

Elizabeth took a couple of deep breaths. It was true. If she wanted information—information and *justice*—this was her chance. She forced herself to back off from the argument. "Later," she told him tersely, staring him in the eye before turning back to Brandon. "I'm sorry if you were misled. I'm sorry if you're disappointed. But we *do* want to hear the truth, and we *do* want to print it. If you're innocent, help us prove it."

"How?"

"Tell us what happened," she urged.

"What happened is that the police turned up one day and arrested me outside my history class." Brandon shook his head in bewilderment as if he still couldn't believe it. "The next thing I knew, I was being charged with murder. But I was framed. I have no idea how Dwayne's stuff got into my locker."

"Start from the beginning," Scott prompted, pulling out chairs for Elizabeth and himself.

Brandon closed his eyes as if he had told the same story over and over and was sick of it. "I'd only been working at the club a couple of weeks. I hardly even knew Dwayne. I had no reason to murder him. None."

"Who did? Any ideas?" Elizabeth asked.

"If I knew, *they'd* be sitting here talking to you and *I'd* be studying for exams right now."

"What do you know about Manoel Coimbra?" Elizabeth asked.

Brandon shrugged. "He was a busboy. Nice kid.

71

From Monterrey, I think. Somewhere in Mexico. Kinda nervous."

"Nervous?" Scott asked.

Brandon nodded. "Yeah. Jumpy."

"Did you ever see Manoel Coimbra and Dwayne together?"

"Just, you know, in the employees' lounge. During breaks."

"Can you remember any conversations between them?" Elizabeth asked. "Did Dwayne ever say anything that appeared to make Manoel nervous?"

Brandon squinted as if he were trying to remember. "Hmmm . . . OK, let's see. The last conversation I remember, Dwayne and I were sitting in the lounge. It was payday. Everybody gets these pay envelopes with their names on them. At any rate, Coimbra walked in, put his pay envelope on the table, and went to get some coffee. When he came back, Dwayne made some remark about the spelling of his name. Coimbra seemed to get real nervous about it."

"Why?" Elizabeth asked.

"Beats me."

"Can you remember what the remark was?" Scott pressed.

Brandon nodded. "Dwayne said something about how weird it was that Manoel spelled his name with an *o* instead of a *u*."

Elizabeth and Scott looked at each other. Scott's face looked blank. They shrugged at each other.

"Did he explain why?" Elizabeth prompted.

"Dwayne said something about Portuguese or

72

Portugal or something." Brandon chuckled mirth-lessly. "Not exactly a motive for murder."

"Liz," Scott began in a low voice. "The obit didn't say anything about Coimbra being from Portugal."

"No," she agreed. "But it *did* say he was from Brazil. And which language do Brazilians speak?"

"Portuguese?"

Elizabeth nodded. She sat back in her chair, her heart beating rapidly. Brandon Phillips was wrong. Whether he knew it or not, Dwayne had provided Manoel Coimbra with a very good motive for mur-der—proof that Manoel wasn't who he said he was. Brandon had been an unwitting witness to the mo-tive . . . and ended up the fall guy.

Dwayne Mendoza knew that Manoel Coimbra—or whatever his real name was—had assumed the identity of a dead man, she realized. *And that knowledge killed him. Why?*

And who will be next?

As chamber music filtered through the air Tom walked across the patio toward the elegant, glassed-in ballroom. Several of the Verona Springs VIPs had already gathered there.

Bunny and Pepper both wore what looked like very fancy dresses. Tight, twisty-looking things in bright greens, pinks, and yellows. The men all wore jackets and ties.

Tom suddenly realized he was seriously underdressed in his black chinos and chambray shirt. Embarrassed, he hurried around the wooden latticework fence that separated the breezeway from the patio. He spotted Carlos walking along the covered walkway that led to the kitchen. "Carlos!"

Carlos stopped and looked around. When he saw Tom, his face closed up slightly. "Yes?" he responded in a wary tone.

He doesn't trust me, Tom thought. *He's afraid he told me too much. And he doesn't want me to ask him any more questions.* "Any chance you could find me a jacket and tie?" he asked in a low voice.

Carlos's face relaxed. "No problem," he said. "Come with me."

Tom followed Carlos into the main entrance of the clubhouse and into the coat check room. Three or four jackets hung at the end of the rod along with an assortment of ties. Carlos took a black-and-tan tweed sport coat from the rack and held it while Tom slipped his arms into the sleeves. "Help yourself. Many gentlemen forget a jacket and tie. So we keep a few on hand." Carlos inspected the ties, chose one, and handed it to Tom. "This one, I think."

Tom nodded approvingly. "You've got good taste. *And* you're a lifesaver." He looped the conservative gray-and-burgundy tie around his neck. "It's important to dress for success, and I want to make a good impression on the congressman."

"Are you going to ask him for a job?" Carlos asked without irony.

Tom hesitated a bit before answering. Did Carlos realize he was a reporter? Would it make any difference to him if he did? Tom looked around but found no prying eyes or ears. With no one watching, Carlos might feel comfortable enough to continue the conversation they had begun in the employees' lounge.

"I'm going to ask him for an interview," Tom answered. "I'm a reporter with WSVU, the campus TV station. And I think I know what's going on around here."

Carlos backed up slightly, and Tom immediately decided to take a chance. Maybe if he took Carlos into his confidence, he could win enough of his trust to get him to speak. "Paul Krandall is shaking you down, isn't he? Blackmailing you and a lot of people who work here?"

"I don't know what you mean," Carlos replied in a guarded tone.

"The money you collected wasn't for some former employee. It was for Paul Krandall."

"You don't know that."

"I *do* know that," Tom insisted. "I *saw* it. Paul had it in the parking lot."

Carlos's breath came in shallow gulps. "The police? Do they know? Is that why they are investigating?"

Tom shook his head. "If the police are investigating, they're looking for a murderer, not illegal immigrants."

Beads of perspiration broke out across Carlos's forehead.

"I'm on your side," Tom told him. "That's why I'm telling you what I know. Because I need your help. I need your help to find out who murdered that caddy. And how Paul—"

The heavy front door swung open with a loud

blam, startling them both. A crowd of people came surging in with a burst of hearty laughter and talk. Carlos hurried out of the cloakroom and Tom followed, curious to see who, or what, was making so much noise.

At that moment Mr. Phelps came through the lobby with a rolling gait right at Tom's shoulder. He navigated the steps of the sunken seating area like a sailor. "Welcome, Congressman Krandall," he boomed. "We're delighted to have you." Mr. Phelps clapped a hand on Tom's back. "And this young fellow here is a reporter from the SVU campus TV station. He's very eager to talk to you, and we're proud and happy that the news will be covering the visit of a distinguished guest to our club."

"Yes, yes," Congressman Krandall bellowed. He was tall, with a red face and white hair, and surrounded by his entourage—a knot of men and women of assorted shapes, sizes, and ages that seemed to move as one. A variety of hands appeared, and Tom wasn't quite sure which one he was supposed to shake.

It didn't seem to matter. The minute he grasped one, he was incorporated into Congressman Krandall's octopal body politic. Fingers squeezed his shoulder. Hands shook his. He was part of the entourage now, moving in lockstep with the others toward the ballroom—while Carlos slipped quietly out of Tom's reach.

Chapter Seven

"You did a great job back there," Scott shouted over the wind.

Elizabeth acknowledged the compliment with a lift of her chin but looked pointedly, silently, at the scenery.

Scott pulled the car over and stopped. "I can't keep shouting at you over the wind." He pressed a button, and the automatic top began to raise.

Elizabeth sat in angry silence while the top closed over them and Scott fastened the ceiling clamps. "You handled that interview like a pro," he said.

"Excuse me if I don't look completely gratified," she said sarcastically. "But I'm not as stupid as you seem to think I am."

Scott's eyes widened as if he were wounded. "What are you talking about?" he gasped.

"You've been complimenting me ever since we left the jail. And I know what you're trying to do. You're trying to smooth my feathers. Feed my ego until I forget that you broke the first rule of collaboration. *Don't lie to your partner.*"

"Elizabeth! I—"

"When you told me to dress conservatively so we could make a good impression at the reception, you were lying. You were manipulating me. You wanted me to dress like this so I could pass for an attorney. Don't you realize how dangerous that little masquerade was?"

"I don't blame you for being angry," he said in a placating voice. "It was definitely a big risk. But it was worth it, wasn't it?"

"I might not have wanted to take that risk," Elizabeth said through clenched teeth. "Did that ever occur to you?"

"Yes," he said calmly. "Which is why I didn't tell you."

"That does it! Of all the things I hate the most, it's people who try to make my decisions for me." Elizabeth jerked the door open and got out of the car. She slammed the door shut as hard as she could and began to pace the gravel shoulder. Tom Watts could be overbearing at times, but he would never have pulled a stunt like this. Never.

Hot tears began to roll down her cheeks. Tears of anger and regret. She and Tom had been so perfect together. Now that they were apart, nothing felt right anymore. *Everything is going so wrong,* she thought miserably. *Everything I do backfires. Maybe I should call him and apologize.*

I need him.

She heard Scott get out of the car. His shoes

crunched along the gravel shoulder. His pace was slow and patient—as if he were prepared to wait out her anger. "I didn't want to put you in the position of having to lie," he said quietly.

"That should have been my decision to make," she managed to say, even though her throat was so tight, she felt as if she might choke.

"Why?" he asked simply.

She whirled around and stared at him. "How can you be so dense? So thick and insensitive?"

"Would Tom have let you make that decision for yourself?" he asked.

"Yes," she answered without hesitation.

"Then he's a coward," Scott said angrily.

"He is not!" she fired back. "He's—" Elizabeth broke off, torn between the desire to defend Tom and to vilify him.

"*I* made the decision—which means *I* assume full responsibility. I was willing to risk *my* neck, but not yours. I would never, *ever* ask a partner to lie or do anything illegal," Scott said.

"But that's exactly what you did."

"No, I didn't. You knew absolutely nothing. If we'd gotten caught or gotten into trouble, you could have sworn, in absolute good conscience, that you had nothing to do with it. In politics it's called 'plausible deniability.'"

Elizabeth's anger began to drain away as the force of his argument sank in.

He smiled wryly. "You could say you were my un-witting dupe. And you would be telling the truth."

"You mean an unwitting *dope?*"

He shook his head. "No, I don't. You are the smartest reporter I've ever met, Liz. I'm not trying to manipulate you. I'm trying to clear the obstacles out of your path and let you do that thing you do." He walked around to the passenger side of the car and opened the door.

Elizabeth removed her black blazer and folded herself into the front seat of the small sports car. When she thought about it in those terms, she realized that Scott was right. Once again she had underestimated him just so she would have a good excuse to romanticize her partnership with Tom.

Scott climbed in the driver's side. "Now. Are you going to tell me what you think? Or do you want to call it quits?"

Elizabeth hesitated.

"Look! You have to make a decision. You trust me or you don't. Either way it's fine with me. I'll even drop you off at WSVU so you can finish this up with Tom if that's what you want. I've kind of had the feeling for a while now that you've been comparing us . . . and I'm coming up short."

Elizabeth felt her cheeks turn scarlet, and she let out a mirthless chuckle. "Did I say you were dense just a moment ago?"

He smiled wryly. "Do you want to finish this story with Tom?"

She thought about that for a moment. If she had been working on this with Tom, there was no way she could have scored the kind of information she had now. While she and Tom had worked side by side, somehow Scott always managed to stay one step ahead of her. And that was exactly the kind of person she needed right now.

"No," she said softly. She meant it.

"You can still dump me," Scott insisted. "I only came on board to satisfy the 'couples-only' rule. There's no law that says you and I have to be the couple. It could be you and Tom."

"I couldn't have gotten this far without you," Elizabeth said truthfully. "I owe you an apology. Sorry." She felt truly guilty.

Scott had uncomplainingly done the heavy lifting and the dirty work to help Elizabeth write *her* story. How could she have doubted he was on her side?

She folded her arms across her chest and leaned her head back against the seat. It was time to move on and get back to work—with Scott, her *real* partner. "OK. Here's how I see it. Whoever that busboy was, he was using phony papers that had been acquired using information from voter registration records and the obits. Happens all the time. Dwayne probably realized that Coimbra wasn't who he appeared to be and that he was an illegal immigrant. I'm guessing he tried to blackmail Coimbra, so Coimbra killed him and framed Brandon."

Scott stared straight ahead, digesting it. "But if he was going to frame Brandon, why split?"

"Because Brandon may have eventually figured it out just like we did. Framing him bought Coimbra time to run. Time to disappear before anybody started looking for him."

"So then he's our murderer. But where is he now?"

Elizabeth shrugged. "I don't know. But we have to find him. There's an innocent man sitting in jail."

And a murderer on the loose, she added mentally, a chill traveling up her spine.

"You brought a different pair of shoes, right?" Lila said. "The basket weave look is totally out of style. They're a weird color too."

"I like these shoes. They're comfortable," Bruce answered. He twisted the steering wheel, positioned his black Porsche in a parking space, and cut the engine.

Lila let out a gasp of impatience. *Honestly!* she thought. *Bruce is getting* so *hard to manage.* "They look horrible," she complained.

"They look fine." He reached over the back of the driver's seat and grabbed his sport coat and tie.

Lila's eyes widened angrily. "I don't believe it. Were you always this passive-aggressive?" She yanked open the door and got out, patting her hair into place.

"Passive-aggressive," he muttered, climbing reluctantly out from behind the wheel. "Where are you coming up with this stuff? You dropped out of Psych 101. You don't know what you're talking about."

Lila watched him shrug on his sport coat. "I'm talking about *this.*" She fingered the material of the jacket with as much contempt as she could muster. "Where did this come from? A chain store, right? It's got low-end merchandising written all over it. Look at the shine on that gab." She reached up and grabbed the collar. "Let me see the label."

Bruce twisted out of her grasp. "It's a navy blazer. It looks like every other navy blazer in the world, Lila. *What* is your problem?"

"Quit it. Just quit it, OK?" Lila was so upset, her hands were shaking. "You're mad about Paul, and you're sabotaging me to get even. Wearing crummy-looking clothes to make me look bad."

"You're crazy!" Bruce's forefinger traced a circle at his temple.

Lila stamped her feet. "I hate it when you play dumb!"

"Who's playing dumb?" He rolled his eyes and shrugged as if he were trying to reason with a lunatic.

"*You* are. You've got a closet *bulging* with expensive menswear. You know the difference between a good piece of fabric and a rag. *Now take that off!*" she finished with a shout.

"Hey, I like this jacket," he said defiantly. When Bruce lifted his hand to straighten his tie, Lila let out another outraged shriek.

"Where is your watch? And what is that . . . that . . . that . . . *thing* on your wrist?"

The timepiece on Bruce's wrist was *not* the unbelievably expensive Giancarlo Colletta limited edition platinum-and-gold watch she had given him for Christmas. It was some cheap novelty watch. A band of black corrugated rubber with a round red face.

Bruce lifted his eyebrows as if he had no idea what she was talking about. He looked all over, then lifted his arm and did a goofy double take when he saw his watch. "Oh!" He brightened. "You mean *this* watch."

"Yeah," Lila said belligerently. "*That* watch!"

"It was a gift," he confided in a pleased tone.

"From who? The gas station?"

"*No*, the dry cleaner. They give 'em away free with every fifty dollars' worth of cleaning." He pointed to the strap. "See? It says 'Thank you for your business. Jeff's Cleaners.'" He held up his wrist and turned it this way and that so he could admire it from every angle. He was acting like a kid thrilled with a cheap toy.

"Take that off."

"No."

"Why are you doing this to me?" she asked tearfully.

Bruce let out an exasperated sigh. "You wanted me to look like a goofball so Paul Krandall could look good, remember? I'm here to serve. You've got my *full* cooperation. Look at me. I'm a *goofball*—complete with a shiny coat and two-cent watch. You should be thrilled. No matter what Paul's wearing, he'll look better than I do."

Lila's lower lip began to tremble. "Why can't you see how important this is to me? Why do you have to embarrass me in front of my friends?" Her shoulders began to shake violently. "I can't . . . I can't . . . I can't *take it anymore*."

"Lila," Bruce begged. "Come on, now. Don't do that."

She opened her mouth and let out a loud, choking sob. "You are *sooo mean*," she wailed, leaning against

84

the roof of the Porsche and pressing her face into her forearms. Lila knew from experience that she could shout at Bruce all day long and get nowhere. It was tears he couldn't cope with. They were incredibly effective, so she tried to use them sparingly. There was always the danger of dulling the effect through overuse. But this situation called for an all-out, ten-hankie blitz.

"Lila! Lila! Please, don't. I'm sorry. I was being mean. I'm really, really sorry." His voice was contrite.

She sobbed louder. "I want to achieve my goal, and you won't help me. You won't even wear the wa-wa-*waaahhhtch* I gave you."

"It's under the seat," he said quickly. "I have it with me. Don't worry, Lila. The Giancarlo Colletta is in the building."

Lila lifted her head and peeped at Bruce as he reached into the car and emerged with the expensive watch dangling from his hand. "I was in a bad mood," he explained, his voice dripping with regret. "I'm sorry. You know I want to help you achieve your goal."

"I had that watch flown here from Italy. Express. So it would be here in time for Christmas," she continued, going for complete and total capitulation. "I put so much thought into it, and you . . . you . . ." Lila let her face crumple piteously and trailed off with a fresh sob.

Bruce fumbled with his novelty watch. "Here. Here. Look." He flung it out into the bushes. "There. It's gone. It never existed." Bruce's fingers expertly fastened the expensive watch around his wrist. "Wow. Look at that. Some watch, huh? I'll bet Paul Krandall's eyes will fall out when he gets a look at that. OK? Are we OK now? Can we stop crying and go in?"

Lila shook her head and fastened her large, tearful gaze on his jacket.

He slipped out of it as gracefully as Gypsy Rose Lee. "Gone," he sang. "It's gone. Bye-bye, rayon. Hello, camel hair." He pressed a button on his key chain and the trunk popped open. Bruce scooped out a sport coat that Lila loved. But it wasn't enough. Not yet.

Lila sobbed louder, pointing down at his shoes. Bruce virtually jumped out of them and dropped them into the well of the trunk.

Lila paused for breath, then shrieked like the ghost of Christmas past.

"All *right*." He retrieved them from the trunk and sent them flying after the watch. They landed in the bushes with a pleasing crash. Bruce rummaged around and produced a pair of Italian loafers. They weren't new, but they had that coveted "distressed money" look.

Satisfied, Lila tapered off a sob and scaled back to a whimper.

Bruce pirouetted like a runway model and tucked his arm through Lila's. "Now, don't we look good together?" He positioned them both so that they could see their own reflections in the black tinted windows of a gray van. Bruce smiled, checking his teeth.

Lila reached into her Julie Tucker clutch bag. It was part of the designer's new Green Collection. Papier-mâché. Shaped like a sea cow. She removed a tissue and dabbed at her nose and eyes. "Please don't put me through anything like this again," she begged.

"I won't," he promised. "I don't know what got into me. I apologize."

"I accept," Lila murmured petulantly. She pulled her arm away from Bruce's clutching fingers and fished around in her sea cow purse for her lipstick and concealer. Crying was hard work, and her face showed it. *Bruce is almost more trouble than he's worth,* she thought as she opened the tiny compact that held her very own, specially formulated concealer.

In the mirror of her compact Lila saw a familiar figure getting out of a car. She turned and waved gaily. "*Hola,* Perdita!"

Perdita waved back. Her heavy gold cuff bracelets gleamed in the sunlight.

"Bruce," Lila began, her eyes narrowing in thought.

"Mmmmm?"

"You know who Perdita reminds me of?"

"Who?"

As Perdita trotted into the club with her boyfriend, Chip, Lila reconsidered telling Bruce who. But he'd *already* accused her of being crazy once today. She didn't want him to accuse her of hallucinating. "Evita Perón," Lila replied quickly, snapping her compact shut. *"La santa Peronista."*

Bruce nodded. "Yeah. There's a definite resemblance, all right. Probably because they're both from Argentina."

"Right," Lila said. *Duh,* she added silently.

Chapter Eight

"Tom! We think the college vote is going to be very important," a short man in a brown suit boomed. He put his hand on Tom's arm.

"Tom!" A woman tightened her hand on the lapel of Tom's jacket and clutched as she made her points. "The congressman *knows* his constituents. He's on *their* side. This is *his* year."

A very young man with a very receding hairline poked his finger into Tom's chest to emphasize his words. "We think the student media is *the single biggest* influence *in* the nation right *now,* and . . ."

The words came out like mortar fire. Tom felt as if he were being pummeled with attention. Battered with slogans.

A heavy hand landed on Tom's shoulder and spun him around. "I would be delighted to visit your studio and chat with you one-on-one," Congressman Krandall offered. He lifted his other big hand and smiled just as the club photographer lifted his camera.

The reception room was almost full now. The Verona Springs members—VIPs and otherwise—had turned out in full force to welcome Paul's father. Noticing that the music had stopped, Tom cast an eye about for Dana.

"Excuse me," he said finally, moving away from the congressman and his glad-handing appendages. "I need to find someone, but I'll check back with you about that interview."

Dana stood in the corner, chatting with two of the musicians. Tom approached her, glad to find someone to talk to who didn't have some kind of agenda. When she looked up and saw him coming, her cheeks flushed, turning a translucent pink, reminding him that Dana *did* seem to have an agenda, far-fetched though it might have been—to get him to fall in love with her. Still, her unstyled mahogany hair and wild clothes made the socialites and politicos look stuffy and conventional while she looked even more beautiful than usual. Perhaps her agenda wasn't so far-fetched after all.

"What did you think?" she asked, lifting her face to look at him.

"I think Congressman Krandall is a phony and a blowhard," Tom said with a laugh.

"Not about him. About the piece. The Schubert." She nudged against him, prodding him to remember.

He ran a hand over the back of his neck. "I'm sorry, Dana. To tell you the truth, there's been so much noise and conversation, I didn't really get a chance to listen."

"That's OK. I'll forgive you on one condition."

"What's that?"

"You give me a kiss for luck." She lifted her face, and Tom bent down, prepared to give her a quick peck. But as he positioned his head she reached up and pulled his head toward hers, kissing him so passionately, he lost his balance. To keep from falling, he leaned forward, pressing Dana against the wall.

That only made her kiss him harder.

"Holy moly!" Jessica exclaimed, her eyes widening at the sight of Tom and Dana in just about the sexiest clinch she'd ever seen this side of a movie screen.

She heard a gasp and saw Lila Fowler less than two feet away. Jessica's heart skipped a beat when she realized that her very American exclamation had caught Lila's attention. *"Ai-yai-yai,"* Jessica amended quickly as Lila's gaze met hers.

Too late. Lila's big brown eyes registered shocked recognition. "Jessica?" she whispered, her eyes growing larger by the second.

Jessica feigned deafness and began squeezing through the crowd toward the other side of the room. Lila had a pretty short attention span. Out of sight, out of mind. *Adiós, Lila!* Jessica thought, trying to get as far out of her best friend's sight as possible.

"Good grief!" Scott breathed as they walked into the reception.

Elizabeth came to a skidding halt when she saw Tom bent over Dana in a passionate kiss. Dana's arms were wrapped around his neck. Tom's hands traveled along Dana's arms and closed around her wrists.

Another frisson of recognition electrified Elizabeth's nerve endings. Tom's hands had traveled along her arms exactly that way, many times.

She squeezed her eyes shut. *Don't watch,* she commanded. *And don't remember!*

But how long would it be before she could see him in another woman's arms without wanting to die? And why couldn't she stop caring? Hadn't he proved over and over that he was a creep? Why couldn't she get it through her head that she and Tom Watts were *over*?

Gently Tom disengaged. When he lifted his head, Elizabeth was directly in his line of vision. His face was flushed, but when his eyes met Elizabeth's, the color drained from his face.

Elizabeth immediately dropped her gaze, then moved with Scott toward the group of people surrounding the congressman. "Come on," Scott whispered. "Let's go meet the big man."

Elizabeth studiously avoided looking over at Dana and Tom, hoping she didn't look as hurt as she felt.

Tom was speechless, embarrassed, and *angry! Why does Dana have to keep pouncing on me in public?* he wondered.

He bit back his irritation. *Be fair, Watts,* he told himself. *You've been giving her green lights all the way.*

Tom felt intensely guilty. He'd told himself that he was using Dana so he could move freely around the Couples-Only areas of the club. But he couldn't help it—Dana just had the power to ring his bells sometimes. Now he was losing control of the situation, and it was all his own fault. He'd treated Dana like a girlfriend, and now she was acting like one.

Dana giggled naughtily. "I thought it was time someone shook this place up a little." She gave the room a little self-satisfied curtsy.

"Excuse me," he told her quietly. "I need some air." Tom didn't wait for her to respond. He quickly slipped out the service door and stood in the breezeway, hoping the cool air would restore his calm. He loosened his tie and ran his fingers through his hair, thinking hard.

For two cents he would drop the whole thing, scamper back to campus, and hunker down in his misery like a wounded dog. But he'd started something with Carlos that he felt duty bound to finish. And in order to do that, he needed help. He needed Elizabeth. Because doing this alone sure wasn't working.

A waiter came out the kitchen door, balancing a large tray of glasses on one hand. The ballroom door opened, and somebody else came out into the breezeway, narrowly missing the waiter. The waiter dodged. The tray swayed precariously. Somehow he managed to avoid collision and continue on with an unruffled smile.

The moving target was that Argentinean girl. Perdita something. "Hi," Tom said, doing his best to smile.

"Hola," Perdita responded. She threw a backward look over her shoulder, as if she were being followed,

then disappeared through the back door of the clubhouse. *"Adiós!"* she yodeled.

A few moments later Lila appeared. "Have you seen . . ." She trailed off and seemed confused.

"Perdita?"

Lila gave him an odd look. "Yes," she answered after a beat. "Right. *Perdita.*"

"She just went into the clubhouse," Tom answered.

Lila smiled. "Thanks." She zoomed through the kitchen doors, obviously mistaking them for the entrance to the clubhouse.

Three seconds later Perdita came out of the clubhouse.

"Lila was just here looking for you," Tom told her, feeling as if he were watching a Marx Brothers movie. "She went in the kitchen."

"Oh, *sí?*" Perdita exclaimed. "Hmmm. Well, if you see *Lee-lah* again, tell her I am not there. *¿Comprende?*" She smiled nervously and scurried back into the reception room.

When the door opened, Tom caught a glimpse of Elizabeth. For once she was standing alone while Scott Sinclair talked to the congressman and some VIPs.

Time to swallow your pride, Watts, he told himself. *If you can get Elizabeth to talk to you, give her what she wants—even if it's your heart on a stake.*

Tom slipped in the door and edged toward Elizabeth. Dana's attention was focused on the congressman. So was Scott's. All clear. Tom managed to inch his way along the wall until he stood right next to Elizabeth.

She turned her head, and he caught a whiff of her perfume. The scent set off a wave of yearning so powerful, he had to fight the urge to fold her in his arms. "I need to talk to you," he said, whispering out of the side of his mouth.

At first he wasn't sure if Elizabeth had even heard him. Then, slowly, she began moving along the wall toward the exit.

"Your investigative style is—how shall I put this—*unusual*," Elizabeth said dryly when they stepped outside. She crossed her arms and lifted her chin. "Actually I think maybe *crude* is the better word."

Elizabeth struggled to keep her voice steady and eyes steely, but it wasn't easy when she had to keep blinking to hold back the tears. She was sick with disappointment and regret. For so long she'd wanted to be alone with Tom. To talk to him and try to tell him how she felt. But it was impossible now. All she could see was him making out against the wall with Dana—at a congressional reception, no less!

At least Tom had the good grace to blush. "That was . . ." He shrugged. "I don't know what that was. OK?"

"Oh, I think I know," Elizabeth said bitterly.

"Then tell me," Tom said.

"I think that between you and Jessica, there is no tactic too low," Elizabeth lashed out. "I can't believe you would use my own sister to pump me for information! And I know what you're doing with

Dana—trying to make me jealous. I guess you think I'm so desperate to get you back, I'll turn over all my notes."

"No," Tom began. "You've got me all wrong. Well . . . OK, some of it you have right. But I'm not out to get you. Really. I'm not."

"Yes, you are," she insisted. "I don't need you anymore, and you can't stand it."

"All right. Have it your way. You don't need me. But I need you."

Elizabeth's heart banged hard in her chest, then skipped a beat. She let out a cry. "No," she choked. "Please . . . don't say anything else." Elizabeth didn't want to hear any more—because in spite of everything that had been said and done, she still wanted to believe him. And every time she believed him, she wound up getting hurt.

Tom stepped toward her. "I need you," he continued, ignoring her pleas. "Not just to help me get this story. I need you to be happy. I miss you."

The cool, dry breeze rustled the potted palms, and Elizabeth felt her resolve bending like their frail stems. When he looked at her the way he was looking now, it was hard to believe he could ever do anything to hurt her. The outside corners of his deep brown eyes turned downward wistfully, and his eyebrows were arched in pained appeal. His lips were parted ever so slightly, just inches away from hers.

"Elizabeth. If we could just talk, you and me . . . maybe we could work things out," he said softly. He lifted his hand to touch her cheek.

Elizabeth swallowed and jerked her head away, not trusting her voice or her emotions. But she couldn't keep either inside. "You were the one who walked away from me," she reminded him. "I offered you a truce in the parking lot yesterday. I told you I'd be straight with you if you'd be straight with me. Funny . . . you didn't seem to need me then."

Tom closed his eyes as if the memory was too painful. "Sometimes I act like a jerk. Sometimes I . . . I get too emotional and I do stupid things. I've *done* some really stupid things, Elizabeth, but the stupidest thing I ever did was break up with you."

Gently Tom moved closer. Elizabeth could smell the starch in his chambray shirt, the faint, soapy smell of his shaving cream. She longed to put her cheek against his.

And she *could*.

Elizabeth leaned toward him, her arms automatically reaching up to circle his neck. Then she found herself jumping away when suddenly the door behind her opened. She whirled around, her face flushing guiltily under Scott's penetrating gaze.

"Problem?" he asked Elizabeth coolly.

Tom clenched his teeth. He'd never disliked anybody quite as much as he disliked Scott Sinclair. He was like Congressman Krandall in there. Too slick. Too practiced. A phony.

Plus Tom really didn't like the proprietary way Scott stood behind Elizabeth with his hand hovering beside her arm. Not touching, but still connecting with it as if he were generating some kind of force field to protect her.

"The only *problem* here is you, pal." The jagged antagonism in Tom's voice cut through the afternoon calm like a chain saw. Elizabeth automatically backed away, her arm fitting perfectly into the waiting curve of Scott's hand.

Tom immediately felt like kicking himself. After all this time apart, he finally had a chance to put things right—and he blew it because he let Scott Sinclair get under his skin.

"Come on," Scott said quietly.

"Elizabeth! Wait! Please," Tom pleaded. "We need to talk. I'm sorry—give me two minutes. Just two minutes."

Elizabeth turned her head. "It's OK," she said to Scott. "I'll come back inside in a minute."

Scott hesitated. He looked back and forth between Tom and Elizabeth as if he was trying to gauge the degree of risk Tom presented. It was almost a parody of protective male behavior. Tom smiled, hoping to lighten the tension. "She's safe with me. I haven't bitten anybody in . . . oh . . . I don't know . . . *days!*"

Tom thought he saw Elizabeth swallow a laugh before composing her face into stern lines.

"I'll be inside if you need me," Scott told her. He leveled a long, warning gaze at Tom before walking back into the ballroom.

When the door closed, Tom rolled his eyes. "Is

97

that the kind of guy you want to work with? Father Knows Best?"

"He takes his responsibilities as a journalist seriously," she said, immediately on the defensive.

"Meaning what?" Tom demanded. "That I don't?"

"Meaning that I'm not willing to sink to your level," she said angrily. "I'm not going to use people to get a story. If you were sorry about us, you had plenty of time to apologize before this. You just want to know what I know? So *say* it! Quit insulting my intelligence by trying to *weasel* it out of me. And quit trying to *romance* it out of me." Her voice broke on the word *romance*.

"OK. I want to know what you know," he said, calling her bluff.

Elizabeth seemed knocked off beam for a moment. She'd obviously expected him to argue that he wasn't just trying to get information, but she quickly recovered. "You go first," she said, giving him a crooked smile.

"Fine. I'll tell you." He walked toward her until they were so close, he could feel the heat coming off her body. "Maybe my piece of the puzzle is the one piece you need to finish it. You can *have* it. You can have the whole story. All I want is a truce." *And you,* he wanted to add. Then he noticed that the door had opened a crack; Scott's blue eye peered out.

"I'm waiting," Elizabeth told him, lifting her chin.

Tom let his arms fall against his sides and snorted with disgust. "What's the use? Whatever I tell you, you'll tell Scott. And there's no way on earth I'm going to let *that* self-aggrandizing truffle pig root out my scoop." Tom yanked the door open and Scott came tumbling out, looking embarrassed to be caught eavesdropping.

"And you think *my* investigative techniques are crude," Tom shot at Elizabeth before walking back into the reception.

Chapter Nine

"Chip? Where did you go to prep?" Paul asked.

Nick took a sip of his soda and racked his brains for the name of a prep school. He'd gone to John D. Killigan, the toughest public high school in Los Angeles. The kind of no-frills school that taught reading, writing, and arithmetic—assuming you could stay alive long enough to learn it. Killigan graduates tended to choose one of two career paths—cop or robber. Nick had been no exception.

"Penceforth Livingston," he improvised, watching a waiter pour a bag of Penceforth-brand pretzels into a serving dish. Livingston, on the other hand, had been the name of the dog he'd had in grade school.

Paul nodded sagely. "An excellent school."

Idiot! Nick thought. Maybe Paul *was* a hustler, as Bruce Patman had insisted. Still didn't mean he had any brains. It didn't take a genius to con this bunch. "What about you?" Nick asked. "Where did you go to prep?"

"Olman," Paul answered. "And my old buddies there have been totally supportive of Dad's campaign. I've contacted several, and they've contributed quite a bit. I'm thinking about a career in campaign fund-raising."

"I'm sure you'd do that very well," Nick murmured. He looked around for Jessica but didn't see her. He'd seen her scurry out of the reception with Lila hard on her heels.

Has Perdita blown her cover again? he wondered, his brow furrowing. If she had, it probably meant his cover was blown too. He wouldn't care, if he hadn't seen Elizabeth arrive with Scott and then disappear out the door with Tom Watts like a pair of coconspirators.

Over Paul's shoulder he saw Tom Watts slip back into the reception. *There's another brain I wouldn't mind picking,* he mused.

Jessica had struck out with Elizabeth this afternoon. But she had insisted that Elizabeth *looked* like she was dying to spill. According to Jessica, she only needed to keep pushing. Nick didn't know if that was true or just wishful thinking on Jessica's part. But if there *was* something to know, he hoped Jessica could get it out of Elizabeth before the student press charged in and gummed up the investigation. It could be dangerous for them and embarrassing to the police.

Where are you, Perdita? he asked silently.

Where are you, Jessica? Lila wondered. She had searched everywhere, determined to get an explanation out of her. She came to a stop outside a ladies' room hidden on the second floor near a banquet room. *Aha!*

"Jessica?" she whispered, opening the door a crack.

There was no answer, but she heard a faint clinking noise inside.

Lila pushed open the door and walked into the spacious and elegantly appointed lounge area. "Jessica? Jessica? Are you in here?" Lila heard the clinking noise again and whirled around. She saw her quarry reaching for the door handle, trying to escape. Lila grabbed the belt of her dress and pulled her back.

"You must have me jumbled up with someone else," the impostor insisted in a heavy, and totally hokey, accent.

"You must have *me* 'jumbled up' with a moron," Lila snapped. "*What* are you doing? And why are you dressed up like that?"

"*Ay,* the dress, she is very fragile. I beg you, release us both."

"Don't even *think* about leaving this ladies' room until you've told me *everything!*"

The woman took off her sunglasses and glared angrily with her trademark sea green Wakefield eyes. Then she threw herself down into a chair in a trademark flouncy Jessica huff. The safety chains on her heavy gold bracelets clinked as she folded her arms across her chest. She crossed her legs and swung one open-toed platform shoe back and forth in agitation. "You could get into big trouble poking your nose where it doesn't belong," Jessica told her.

"Let's leave my nose out of this. What are you doing in a club where *you* don't belong?"

"I can't answer that question," Jessica told her

stubbornly. "Now let's just forget you ever saw me."

Lila conjured up a mental picture of Chip. Take away the glasses, muss the hair, change the clothes, and . . .

"What's Nick doing here?" she asked. A horrible suspicion began to dawn. "Does it have anything to do with Paul? Did Bruce call Nick and whine about Paul hustling him?" Lila could practically see her VIP dreams going up in smoke.

Jessica rolled her eyes. "Oh, puh-*leeze*. Like the police have nothing better to do than worry about Bruce and his stupid ego."

Lila was tired of Bruce and his stupid ego too, but she didn't know where Jessica got off running Bruce down—especially since she wasn't even a member of the club. "I thought the police were supposed to protect people," Lila said tartly, determined to take Jessica down a peg. "Bruce is a person."

"Do you think we *ought* to investigate Paul?" Jessica countered immediately, her eyes lighting up.

Lila dropped it like a hot potato. She enjoyed needling Jessica—but not enough to risk creating some kind of trouble for Paul. "Of course not. I just don't know why you can't tell *me*, your *very best* friend, what's going on."

Jessica sighed. "I don't really know what's going on."

"Yeah, right."

"It's the truth. The police had some questions about something that happened here a while ago, and we're checking it out. But so far we haven't found anything. And that's the truth."

Lila bit her lip. "Something that happened *before* Bruce and I started coming here?"

"Maybe."

"So it wouldn't be anything that would affect us? I mean . . . our becoming VIPs?"

"Doubt it."

Lila's anger and worry vanished. "Well, then, if it doesn't have anything to do with me or Bruce, it's not all that important, is it?" She opened her little sea cow purse and reached for her lipstick. "But remember, when you *can* talk about it, I'm your best friend, so *I* get to hear everything *first*. OK?"

Jessica opened her own purse and removed a lipstick brush. "OK. But only if the information's not, like, *classified* or something."

"I thought you said you didn't have any information," Lila challenged.

"I don't."

"Then quit showing off and acting important," Lila snapped. "Now come on. We have to get back to the reception. I want to make sure Congressman Krandall knows my dad is George Fowler, as in Fowler Enterprises."

"And you accuse *me* of showing off and acting important."

"Well, I *am* important," Lila told her with a giggle. "So why *shouldn't* I show off?"

"I'll never forget that match if I live to be a hundred," Anderson Pettigrew drawled. "Mack the Hack here set the world record for double faulting."

Anderson opened his mouth, and his loose, rosy lips quivered as he whinnied.

Bruce smiled tightly and fought the urge to imitate him right to his face.

"If it hadn't been for Lila, I don't think you guys would have scored a single point." Bunny opened her big mouth and brayed. *Hee-haw. Hee-haw.* Like a donkey.

Bruce couldn't believe he'd ever gone out with her, even if it *had* been a blind date. She had the biggest, whitest teeth he'd ever seen. On purpose! That was the part that really blew Bruce away. She'd actually *paid* somebody to paste those suckers on. The whole Sterling family had teeth like that. Her mother. Her father. Her two sisters. They were all very Hollywood. Big hair. Big teeth. Big house in Hollywood Hills.

"Mack the Hack," Pepper tittered. "I love it. Don't you love it, Bun?"

Hee-haw. Hee-haw. Bunny nodded. Up. Down. Up. Down. "I love it, Pep."

Anderson began singing "Mack the Hack" to the tune of "Mack the Knife." Some of the other VIPs joined in. Every time they sang the words "Mack the Hack," they pointed at Bruce and roared with laughter.

Bruce wished that some thoughtful sniper would just put a bullet in his back and save him from further humiliation. He gazed absently over the top of Pepper's teased and laminated blond crown and noticed Paul and his father talking with some of the campaign entourage. Paul held the silver trophy in his hands and turned it this way and that, admiring it as he conversed. Bruce gagged.

Just behind Paul, Lila and Perdita emerged through the back door. Lila lifted her fingers, fluttered them in his direction, and wove her way through the crowd—toward Paul and his father.

Bruce clenched his teeth. *Why is Lila so determined to get in good with this bunch of bozos?* he fumed. *So they're rich! Big deal. Lila's richer than they are. They ought to be chasing* her. But the minute Lila caught the Verona Springs VIP bug, she had turned into a different person. A total snob monster.

Meanwhile Anderson & Co. had launched into another verse.

I don't need this, he thought. *I'm outta here.* But when Bruce tried to walk away, Anderson took his sleeve and drew him back, insisting that he sing along. Bruce was in the process of balling his hand into a fist when the high-pitched shriek of an amplified mike brought him up short.

Everybody stopped their conversation as a bouncy arrangement of "We're in the Money" blasted through the room, segueing into a couple of bars of "Hail to the Chief."

A huge burst of laughter erupted from the congressman's corner, and after a few moments a member of his entourage turned off the canned music and handed Congressman Krandall the microphone.

The congressman's face never lost its genial smile as he waited for the rustles and murmurs to die away. When he looked out across the sea of faces, he seemed to make eye contact with each and every person in the room.

Professional sincerity, Bruce thought, his stomach turning.

"Thank you for coming today. It's a pleasure to be here and meet my son's friends. I can see why he speaks so highly of you all."

His florid remarks earned him a round of enthusiastic and appreciative applause. He bowed slightly, acknowledging it. "As I'm sure you all know, I'll be running for reelection in the coming months."

The crowd applauded and whistled.

"I know also that you young people are eager to participate in the democratic process. By voting. By campaigning. *And by contributing.*"

The room was quiet as everyone listened attentively, nodding solemnly as he spoke.

"I'll cut to the chase, as you young people like to say. Campaigns cost money. Part of my job is to ask people like you to vote with your checkbooks."

Bruce couldn't believe it. This group was the crassest bunch of money clutches he'd ever come across. They were actually going to pass the hat! How low-rent could you get?

A few feet away he watched Lila open her little sea cow purse and pluck out a folded-up check.

Bruce could feel a slow burn starting. He met Lila's eyes and glared, telegraphing his question with his body language. *So, Lila, how come you didn't tell me Congressman Krandall was going to put the bite on everybody?*

Lila smiled smugly and winked. Her body language answering in true Lila fashion, *Because I was afraid you would refuse to come, and I wanted you to.*

Well, Lila was one hundred percent right about that. He *would* have refused. But now that he was here, he was going to refuse to pay. He smiled and winked back at her.

She dimpled like a child who had been naughty but knew she'd get away with it because she was just *sooo* doggone *cute.*

As Paul Krandall stood beside his father, holding aloft the silver trophy he had "won," Bruce felt the little vein in his right temple begin to throb.

Ha! he thought viciously. *Lila can cry me a river for all I care. But not one more Patman dollar is going into the Krandall family coffer.*

Lila sidled over and stood next to Bruce. She lifted her eyes and looked at him from beneath her lashes, smiling sweetly. He smiled down at her, feeling happy for the first time in several days. Any second now Bruce was going to drop it on her, Paul, and the whole VIP jackal pack.

The silver trophy was passed from hand to hand so people could drop their checks in it. Bruce bounced slightly on his toes, anticipating his big moment. When the silver trophy was handed to Bruce, he handed it directly to Anderson. "I'm not making a contribution," he said loudly, enjoying a very Patrick Henry–like feeling of righteous rebellion.

Bunny and Pepper gasped.

"What's the matter, Mack?" Anderson drawled. "Aren't you a Krandall supporter?"

"Of course he is," Lila said quickly.

"No, I'm not," Bruce argued, rocking cockily on his heels.

"He's being funny," Lila explained.

"No, I'm not," Bruce said again. "I'm serious. I'm not giving that guy a dime."

"Bruce!" Lila stamped her foot.

Bruce's own genial smile disappeared, and he felt his eyebrows meet over the bridge of his nose. "I'm not caving in," he said to Lila. "Not this time. Not anymore."

In spite of his misery over Elizabeth, Tom couldn't help but laugh at the conversation taking place behind him. *Good for Patman,* Tom thought. *I didn't know he had it in him.*

"Bruce," Lila insisted angrily. "It's for a good cause."

"Yeah, right," Bruce answered sarcastically. "Like son, like father. They invite you into a dark alley for a friendly game of tennis and then *bammo!* they mug you. I've already written one big check to Paul Krandall Junior. That's it. No more."

A check! Tom's heart skipped a beat. *A check?* His mind raced, trying to absorb this new piece of information. If Bruce wrote Paul a check, then the money Paul had was *certainly* the money that had been collected from the workers in the employees' lounge. *But how can I prove it?*

"Maybe Bruce can't afford to make a contribution,"

Paul said with a silly, grinning attempt at a sneer. He reached into his pocket and removed a wad of cash. "Here, Patman. Let me help you out with a few bucks." He peeled a few bills off the wad and handed them toward Bruce.

Bruce looked at the money in Paul's hand for a long, long time. There was a tense, hushed silence in the room as everyone waited for the explosion. Tom readied himself to step in and break it up if it came to blows.

Finally Bruce plucked the bills from Paul's hand and put them in his pocket. "Thanks," he said brightly.

Everybody in the room let their breath out at once, and several people erupted into nervous laughter.

Tom squinted hard at the wad of money left in Paul's hand. When he saw the word *suerte,* his heart began to hammer. That bill was evidence of extortion. It wasn't solid, but Tom would find a way to prove it in a court of law. He'd find a way for Carlos and for every other Verona Springs worker being held down under Paul's thumb.

"Need any more?" Paul asked, his thumb pressing against the ten-dollar bill and obscuring two letters of *suerte.* "Don't be shy about asking. That's what friends are for."

Tom held his breath. Once that bill left Paul's possession, there would be no way to prove he was running a shakedown operation.

Bruce chewed his lip as if he were thinking it over.

Say no! Tom willed mentally. *Say no. You've gotten your laughs. Say no!*

"No, thanks," Bruce said lightly. "If I need any more, I'll call you."

Tom felt his shoulders sag with relief. The group around Bruce began to giggle and whisper as Paul stalked away.

Trying his best not to break into a run, Tom headed for the service door. He had to find Carlos and get him to cooperate. If he would be willing to make a statement under oath, they could probably have Paul in jail by dinner.

Once outside, Tom ran along the breezeway. He yanked open the kitchen doors and hurried in. Gleaming chrome shelves, steamer trays, and grills filled the enormous kitchen. Since it was between mealtimes, the place was virtually empty.

Tom's breath came in shallow gulps. His heart hammered. He had to hurry. There wasn't much time. Paul could leave and spend the bill. Tip somebody with it. Hand it to his dad. Anything could happen.

A young Latino busboy came in carrying a plastic tub full of glasses and silverware. He gave Tom a shy smile and began putting the things in the enormous, industrial-size dishwasher.

"Where is Carlos?" Tom demanded.

The busboy shook his head.

"What's your name?" Tom asked.

The young man looked blank.

"You were in the employees' lounge the day Carlos collected the money, weren't you?" Tom asked. He knew it wasn't fair to pull this young man into something that might get him in trouble, but Tom didn't have a choice. In the long run it would be worse to allow Paul to continue blackmailing people.

The young man stared at Tom, his forehead creased in a frown.

Tom tried to slow down. "The other day? Remember? You gave Carlos some money. Right?"

The boy shook his head, obviously unable to understand what Tom was telling him. Tom wished he'd taken Spanish instead of French.

"Stay here," he begged. "OK? ¿Comprende? Stay here."

Tom ran out the kitchen door, hoping the young man had understood. He had to find somebody to translate.

He had to find Perdita.

Jessica began moving toward the door and lifted her finger to catch Nick's eye. She needed to let him know that Lila had recognized her—and him too. Lila could probably be trusted not to say anything, but deciding whether or not to continue the investigation wasn't up to her. It would have to be Nick's call. *It takes me a while to learn,* she thought ruefully. *But once I get it, I've got it.*

Nick was looking in the opposite direction. She lifted her arm to wave again and a hand closed over it. Jessica reflexively pulled away, but Tom tightened his grasp on her upper arm. "I need you," he said curtly. He began pulling her toward the service door.

"But . . . b-but . . . ," she sputtered, trying to

collect her thoughts. What was Tom up to? Was he on to her too?

"Don't ask me questions. I don't have time to answer. Just come on."

Her high heels clattered on the pavement of the breezeway.

"It won't take long," Tom insisted. "You can go back to the reception in two minutes." He pushed open the door to the kitchen. "I just need you to translate something. Please."

Jessica's throat tightened, and she dug in her heels. *Oh no!* "I am so sorry, but I am late for a dental appointment and—"

But Tom kept pulling, and Jessica's shoes skidded on the kitchen floor like ice skates.

"It'll only take a second. I swear."

Jessica put a hand to her cheek and moaned. "Ohhh, the pain. I cannot think for the pain. *Owww!*" Her cry of pain was genuine. She was painfully *humiliated*.

Nick is going to kill me, she thought miserably. *Or else he's going to laugh himself silly.* It was bad enough having to admit that *Lila* spotted her. Never mind Tom. By the time she got out of the reception, the entire VIP Circle would probably know she was an imposter.

A young man stood alone in the kitchen. He wore a soiled white apron and appeared to be a busboy.

"Please, Perdita, ask him if he remembers the day Carlos collected money from the employees in the lounge," Tom instructed.

113

The young man looked at Jessica and Tom with big, curious eyes.

"Go ahead," Tom urged. "Ask him."

Jessica opened and closed her mouth. What could she do? She was a D-grade Spanish student—on a *good* day. "Ummm . . . my English, she is not so good," she said to Tom. "Have to go now. *¡Adiós!*" She started toward the door, but Tom pulled her back.

"No. Really. It's simple. Just ask him if he remembers the day Carlos collected money."

Jessica exchanged a nervous glance with the young man. "*El* dee-*say que . . . rememberado el dinero* . . . ummm . . . *a la playa . . .*"

The young man frowned in confusion at Jessica's "Spanish." He listened intently, as if he were honestly trying to figure out what she was saying.

"*Lo siento,*" he began.

"*¡Silencio!*" A different male voice demanded firmly.

The young man jumped. They all did.

"Carlos!" Tom said in a voice of relief. "Thank goodness you're here."

Despite Tom's friendly greeting, the man who stood in the kitchen doorway watched them with angry eyes. He jerked his head toward the door, and the busboy hurried from the kitchen with his eyes on the floor.

Carlos's dark, brooding gaze followed him. When he was sure the busboy was out of earshot, he walked slowly toward Tom and Jessica.

Tom let go of Jessica's arm, and she swallowed nervously. Had this Carlos guy overheard her ridiculously inept attempt to speak Spanish?

114

Carlos seemed to think carefully before speaking. He wiped his hands on a white cloth, then wadded it up and placed it on the counter. "It is not wise to ask questions," he said finally.

Tom stepped toward him. "I can help."

Carlos shook his head. "It is dangerous to ask questions. Dangerous for *you*," he repeated, looking Tom straight in the eye. His gaze held Tom's without wavering for a long, long moment.

Jessica realized she was holding her breath. Afraid that if she exhaled, the noise might draw attention to her.

Tom turned his head slightly and watched Carlos out of the corner of his eye. "What, exactly, are you telling me?"

Carlos never blinked. "I'm telling you, for your own safety, to go back to the party. Then go home. And don't come back." He turned to leave, then seemed to remember Jessica.

Her palms began to sweat when he turned his face toward her. "I forgot. The lady does not speak very good English." Carlos smiled politely at Jessica. *"Te digo para su propia seguridad—regrésate a la fiesta. Luego véte a la casa y no regresas."* He concluded his speech with a waiterly bow and left the kitchen.

Tom stared at the door, the muscles in his jaw working. "I don't get it," he muttered to himself. "Was he *warning* me? Or was he *threatening* me?"

"Oh, good," Jessica said, exhaling in relief. "I didn't get it either. I thought I was just being dense."

Tom's eyes bulged out of their sockets. "Jessica!"

115

Jessica groaned, lifted her wrists, and banged her gold cuffs against her forehead. When would she learn to stay in character? *"Adiós,"* she chirped, pirouetting toward the door, her forties-style fluted hem fluttering around her knees.

"Not so fast, *Perdita*." Tom grabbed her arm, marched her over to a chair, and pushed her into it. He studied her in the light. Finally he whistled. "Unbelievable," he marveled.

"Pretty good disguise, huh?" she squeaked.

"I'll say. But why?"

"I can't tell you why," Jessica responded. "So please don't ask. And please don't tell Nick you recognized me. He'll never let me go undercov—oh, *pretzels!*"

Tom pulled up a chair and sat down across from her. "You're here with Nick? Working undercover? What are you investigating?"

"What are *you* investigating?" Jessica countered. "And what is *Elizabeth* investigating? I'll show you mine if you show me yours. Or hers, or . . . whatever."

Tom's face closed up slightly. "It doesn't work that way."

"I didn't think so." Jessica hopped up, eager to escape before she accidentally told Tom anything else. "Well, then, gotta cha-cha-cha. Later!"

"Jessica—"

"Hush with the Jessica!" she shouted. "I am Perdita del Mar, mysterious woman of, uh, mystery!"

No, I'm not, she thought resignedly as she left the kitchen, running. *OK, Nick, you win. I'm a washout at undercover work. This investigation has officially tanked.*

Chapter
Ten

"I'm never speaking to you again," Lila said. Never, in her whole life, had she been so humiliated. She quickened her step, hurrying to the Porsche ahead of Bruce.

"I'm sorry," Bruce said in a steely tone. He pressed his key chain. A discreet electronic squeak announced that the doors were unlocked.

Lila waited for Bruce to catch up so he could open it for her. But Bruce opened the driver's side door and climbed in.

She yanked the passenger door open and shut it with a *slam*. Not content to humiliate her, he was now adding insult to injury. He wasn't even going to act like a gentleman and open the door for her.

She sat in her contoured bucket seat, panting with indignation. "I can put up with a lot of things," she said, struggling to keep her voice steady. "I can put up with a bad temper. A slob. A louse. Or a liar. But I will *not* put up with a *cheapskate!*"

Bruce banged his fist against the steering wheel. "I resent that. Look at this." He pressed a button, and Lila's seat moved up and down like a dental chair. "Do you know what that option cost me? Do you have any idea? It cost a bundle."

"Stop doing that," Lila snapped. "It makes me carsick."

Bruce reached over and opened the glove compartment. Attached to the upper part of the box was a small computer unit with blinking lights and spinning needles. "State of the art," Bruce announced. "That's a McDougal Donner–designed computer-guided copilot system. We get lost in the middle of the sub-Sahara? No problem. This baby guides us right out of there."

Lila slapped the glove compartment shut with her knee. "Who cares?" she yelled. "We're not *going* to the sub-Sahara. For sure not in *this* car. We *did* have a shot at going to the White House. But nooo," she said sarcastically. "Mr. Patman is *not* going to Washington. He's too principled. And too *cheap!*"

If she hadn't already cried once today, she would have burst into tears. Instead she stared miserably down at her sea cow purse. Bruce had effectively revoked her bragging rights around the sorority house. Knowing Jessica, she would brag for the next five years about her "undercover work with the police." Lila wouldn't be able to brag about anything at all—not unless she wanted to brag about having the world's biggest dolt for a boyfriend.

Bruce started the engine, and his sleek car pulled out

of the parking lot and onto Verona Springs Highway.

Lila angrily watched the scenery pass as the car whizzed along toward the turnpike. Sweet Valley was five miles to the right. The Verona Springs Reservoir was several miles to the left.

She'd heard Pepper and Bunny laugh about VIP nighttime swimming parties held at the reservoir. Parties that were too wild to be held at the club or at home. It seemed highly unlikely that she or Bruce would be invited to any VIP parties now.

The thought of so many lost opportunities enraged her beyond description. She looked over at Bruce's profile. Lila couldn't believe she had ever thought he was good-looking. He wasn't. He looked *stupid!* His nose was a funny shape. His chin was weak. And she didn't like his hair parted on the right like that.

Suddenly Lila realized she was falling out of love. Feature by feature.

His cheeks were too puffy. His eyelashes were too sparse.

He tugged his earlobe and waggled it, obviously trying to relieve an itch inside his ear canal. *Gross!* That move made Lila sick to her stomach.

"So," he said after they had driven a couple of miles in silence. "What do you want to do now? Get something to eat?"

That was one of the things she hated the most about Bruce. He seemed to have a hard time understanding that when she got mad, she *stayed* mad. Just because she hadn't been yelling for the last five minutes didn't mean she wasn't furious.

119

"I want you to take me home," she announced. "And then I want you to drive away and never call me again."

"Oh, Lila," Bruce whined. "You don't mean that." He reached over to try to take her hand.

She angled her sea cow purse and shut it on his fingers.

"Ouch!" he yelled. He turned his amazed and hurt gaze on her. "Are you crazy?"

"Watch the road," she reminded him.

He steadied the car. "Lila. Honey. Sweetcakes. Come on. You can't *really* be that mad at me."

"I am that mad at you," she said. "And we're through. I'm not going to stay in a relationship with somebody who won't take me seriously and help me achieve my goal."

Bruce let out a long-suffering sigh. Lila could tell he didn't quite believe her. *You'll believe it when I stop taking your phone calls,* she thought spitefully.

"So you're saying you want to what? Break up?" he asked.

"Hello-o!" she said. "*I'm* going back to the club. *I'm* going to become a Verona Springs VIP. You can go hang out with your pal Jeff, the dry cleaner. Get a new watch. You don't deserve a Giancarlo Colletta." She grabbed for his wrist.

He pulled his arm out of her reach, smiling. "You have to be part of a couple to go back," he reminded her.

Lila smiled her most malevolent smile. "That's right," she responded in a honeyed voice. "And you know what? I don't think Bunny has been making Paul too happy lately."

"What!" he yelled. He snapped his head to the right to look at her, and the car veered into the wrong lane.

"Watch it!" Lila cried.

Bruce spent the next twenty seconds trying to avoid a head-on collision. "You're just yanking my chain," he said when he had the car under control.

"No, I'm not," she argued.

"You'd never date Paul Krandall." He chuckled in a cynical, knowing, you-can't-fool-me way that only strengthened her determination.

"Just watch me."

"It's not funny!" Jessica insisted.

But Nick pounded the steering wheel, convulsing with laughter. "Yes, it is," he wheezed. "I'd give a month's pay to have seen you dodging Lila and trying to translate for Tom." He laughed so hard, the car almost veered into the wrong lane.

Jessica stared out the window, her cheeks burning with embarrassment. "You told me I should tell you if there was something you needed to know. I did. So why are you making fun of me?"

"Hey!" he said, trying to get his laughter under control. "Don't look like that." Nick reached over and took her hand. "You're good at disguising yourself. Your instincts *were* good. I'm not laughing at *you*. I'm laughing at the situation." Nick squeezed her hand. "Don't be embarrassed. Nine out of ten undercover ops are a waste of time. Welcome to the exciting world of police work, Jess."

"I'm still bummed."

"That's cool," Nick told her. "Be bummed, but get over it. That's how you keep your mental health. You also have to laugh." He grinned at her. "Come on, *Perrrdita*. Laugh. You know you're dying to."

The corners of Jessica's mouth twitched, and she giggled.

"There you go," he said approvingly.

"But it's *not* a waste of time," Jessica insisted. "Tom Watts and my sister are both good reporters. If they think there's something going on at the club, then something is going on."

Nick reached up and messed his carefully combed hair. "I'm sure they do. But it's probably wishful thinking. Reporters always hope they can find a story. They spend a lot of time on wild-goose chases."

"What about Carlos?" she asked. "What about that conversation?"

Nick blew out his breath. "I dunno. It's strange. But it could mean anything. It could mean the kitchen staff is tired of having student reporters underfoot. I think that at this point, all we can do is report to the chief and sign ourselves out on this one."

"Bummer."

"Get over it," Nick growled in mock anger.

"Ready to go?" Tom asked Dana.

She zipped her cello into its large leather case while her fellow musicians gathered up their music and instruments. The reception was almost over. Most of the club members had left or drifted out to the patio dining area.

"We can eat dinner here if we want," Dana told him. "It's part of the deal."

The last thing Tom wanted to do was sit out on the patio with Carlos watching him. "I've got to get back to the station," Tom said apologetically.

Dana pushed her long hair back off her forehead. "You're mad about the kiss, aren't you?" She laughed.

"I'm not mad," he answered. "It was a great kiss."

She smiled. "In case you hadn't noticed, I'm not like Elizabeth. At all. I'm very spontaneous."

"Spontaneity is a good quality."

She leaned her head against the instrument and peered up at him. "Do you ever do things spontaneously?"

"Every Tuesday at four," he quipped.

She smiled, but her eyes made it clear she was still waiting for a real answer.

Once again Tom had the uncomfortable feeling that the conversation was taking him somewhere he didn't want to go. He felt a little flicker of resentment in his chest. Why couldn't she just say what she had to say? He didn't have time to play twenty questions with her every time they got together. "Sure," he said. "Sometimes I do."

"Then how about a swim at the Verona Springs Reservoir?" she suggested. "And a picnic."

"Great. When?"

"Now?" She lifted her eyebrows.

Tom cleared his throat. "I'd really love to do that sometime," he said, feeling irritated at being cornered. "But I really can't—not tonight. I've got to get back to the station. Maybe another day?"

The shrug of her thin shoulders seemed to be telling him that her suggestion had been a now-or-never invitation. Tom knew what was going on. Her feelings were hurt, and she was challenging him to demonstrate his interest in her. But Tom couldn't play that game with her tonight. Jessica and Nick had left twenty minutes ago, and he was itching to get going. He had a plan to find out what they were up to, and he couldn't pursue it until he could get out alone.

"I've got some stuff that just won't wait," he said, trying to be diplomatic. "But I really, really do hope we can do it another time."

After a long pause she seemed to think better of her take-it-or-leave-it offer. Her petulant face broke into a sunny smile. "Sure," she chirped. "Maybe next Tuesday at four."

He smiled back, glad it wasn't turning into a deal breaker. "Do you want me to drive you back to campus?" he asked, hoping she would say no.

"No, thanks. I've got my housemate's Plymouth, so I think I'll hang around and have dinner with the others." Dana swayed forward and brushed her lips against his. "See you," she said before lifting her cello and backing out the door with it.

Tom went over to Congressman Krandall, who was sitting at a table with Paul and several of his entourage. "Good-bye, sir. It was . . . a pleasure."

Congressman Krandall jumped to his feet and extended his hand. "Thank you for coming," he boomed in his big deep voice. His hand tightened around Tom's while his other hand kneaded Tom's upper arm. "And I'll look forward to hearing from you about that interview. Tom, I think the college vote is going to be very important. I *know* my constituents. I'm on *their* side. This is *their* year. The student media is *the single biggest* influence *in* the nation right *now*, and . . ."

Tom had heard all this before, and he really didn't want to hear it again. He managed to extract his hand before the congressman cranked into full gear. "That's great. I'll get in touch through Paul." He backed away, waving and smiling.

Paul and his father waved and smiled too.

Tom's big smile was still frozen on his face when he stepped out the door. A passing waiter, seeing his friendly smile, returned it. "Hello!" he said brightly.

Anderson and Pepper saw him and waved and smiled.

Tom waved and smiled back. And waved. And smiled. And waved. And smiled . . . until he got to the parking lot.

He had to restrain himself to keep from running to his car. He unlocked the door and reached under the seat. Police scanners were contraband; not even Elizabeth knew he had one. But if Nick and Jessica thought it was worth coming to the club undercover, the scanner might give him some clue as to why.

*   *   *

Lila hurried into her room, kicking off her high-heeled mules as she reached for the telephone and her phone book. She sat on the bed, flipping the pages until she found the number she was looking for. The Verona Springs ballroom.

Someone answered on the second ring. "Verona Springs ballroom."

"Is Paul Krandall there?" she asked.

"Junior or Senior?" the voice inquired.

"Junior," she answered.

"Just a minute, please."

Lila crossed her legs and jiggled her foot nervously.

"Hello?" Paul's voice sounded even more adenoidal over the phone than it did in person.

"Hi. It's Lila. I'm so upset, I just had to call and apologize for Bruce's behavior. I hope your father wasn't insulted."

"Gosh, no," Paul responded. "I explained about Bruce. How he's got a couple of screws loose."

Lila licked her lips nervously. "Does your dad know who my father is?" she asked. "Did you tell him?"

"I sure did, and he was really thrilled by the size of your contribution," Paul answered.

"I'd like to do more," she said solemnly. "My father is very interested in making sure we get the best government money can buy." She frowned. Was that actually what she meant? Oh, well . . . She plunged on. "And . . . well, um . . . I'd sure love to have an opportunity to talk about politics and stuff with him."

"Why don't you come back to the club and have dinner with us," he suggested. "On the patio."

"I don't want to intrude."

"You're not intruding. Not at all," he insisted. "It'll just be you, Dad, me, Bunny, and some of Dad's team."

"Oh," Lila said in a flat tone.

There was a pause. "Actually . . . I think Bunny may have to leave soon," he added in an exploratory tone.

Bruce was right. Paul wasn't as dumb as he seemed. "Oh," she repeated, infusing the word with lilting enthusiasm this time.

"Yeah. I'm *sure* she has to go home," he added.

Lila heard a sudden squawk of feminine protest in the background. "Ommmpj . . . suhrubllt . . . gbon't go rhjome." Bunny's garbled voice rose, and then the sound damped out completely. Lila hoped Paul had completely covered the receiver with his hand so he could tell Bunny to scram.

Don't feel too bad, Bunny. You can have Bruce back. You two deserve each other. She covered the mouthpiece at her end so Paul couldn't hear her giggling at the prospect. By tomorrow morning she was going to be Paul Krandall's girlfriend, and Bunny would be VIP history.

"So jump into something eveningish and come on back," Paul told her, coming back on the line. "We'll have dinner out by the pool."

"See you soon," Lila cooed. She hung up the phone and drummed her fingers on her jawline for a moment before springing into action. What should she wear? She dashed to her closet and pawed through her clothes, selecting pewter satin pajama pants and a

127

strappy halter top. Then she changed her mind. It was too bare. She put it back in the closet and removed a soft white muslin blouse and slim black slacks.

She held the blouse up to the light. Nope. Too sheer.

She sighed, wondering if her book on etiquette would have any useful advice as to how much skin it was proper to show when dining with a representative of the U.S. Government.

Realizing she didn't have time to look it up, Lila pulled out a short-sleeved green dress with a nipped-in waist and full skirt. That would be perfect. And it was a good green on her. *Sort of money green,* she thought happily.

Bruce loosened his tie as he got out of his Porsche in front of Sigma house. Fights with Lila were just *exhausting*. And this one had left him feeling strangely unsettled. Would she really make good on her threat to date Paul Krandall?

Winston Egbert came bopping by on his ten-speed and braked with the toes of his high-top sneakers when he saw Bruce. "Who died?" he asked, pointing to Bruce's tie and jacket.

"Very funny, Winston. For your information, I've been at the Verona Springs Country Club."

Winston pursed his lips and whistled. He let his hand hang limply from his wrist and wagged it. "Impressive," he said. "Are you joining?"

Bruce grimaced. "No way. Those guys are too snobby, even for me."

Winston reared back behind his wire-rimmed glasses as if he found it hard to believe that anything, or anybody, was actually *too snobby* for Bruce.

Bruce rolled his eyes. Winston was just one of those people who seemed *compelled* to mock their betters. Normally Bruce would have depressed his pretensions with one of his classic sneers and walked off with his nose in the air. But right now he needed a little reassurance. "Got a minute?" he asked Winston.

Winston reared back even farther. "Bruce Patman wants to talk to *me?*"

"Sure, why not?"

"You want the reasons listed alphabetically or in ascending order of importance?"

Bruce smiled. "We don't have much in common, but we're both men. Right?"

Winston nodded. "Uh . . . yeah?"

"We're both men with girlfriends. So that give us a bond. A common experience."

"So what's your point?"

Bruce leaned back against his Porsche and patted it, indicating he wanted Winston to join him. "I need advice," he admitted.

Winston jumped off his bike and dropped it like a man who had just received a shocking piece of news. "Bruce Patman wants advice from *me?*"

Bruce ignored the sarcasm. It was beneath him to notice. Responding would just encourage Winston. Besides, Bruce really *did* want to talk. "You and Denise fight sometimes, right?"

Winston nodded. "Of course." He leaned against

the Porsche without really leaning against it, as if he thought Bruce's invitation was some kind of cruel trick.

"You always make up and get back together, right?"

"So far," Winston confirmed.

"Has she ever said she never wants to see you again?"

Winston stared into space. "I don't *think* so," he mused. "Not in those words exactly."

"What about . . . 'Never call me again,'" Bruce pressed. "Has she ever said that?"

Winston's tongue poked out of the side of his mouth while he searched his memory. "No. No, I don't think she's ever told me not to call her again."

Beads of perspiration broke out along Bruce's hairline. "'We're through'? How about that one?"

"Nope!" Winston replied. "Why do you ask?"

"Lila and I had a fight. She got pretty mad and said some things I'm sure she didn't mean."

"She said she never wants to see you again, don't call her, and you guys are through?" Winston asked.

Bruce nodded. "Pretty much. But I don't think she was serious."

Winston tugged at the neck of his T-shirt and chewed on it for a few moments. "I don't know, Bruce. If I were you, I think I'd be worried. That sounds pretty serious."

Bruce began to feel better. "This is great." He slapped Winston on the back. "This is exactly what I need you to do."

"What am I doing?"

"You're playing devil's advocate so I can see how

ridiculously unfounded my concerns are."

"But . . . I'm *not* playing devil's advocate," Winston insisted. "I think you got a problem, Houston."

"No way," Bruce argued. "Lila didn't mean it. She couldn't." He began to laugh. "Can you believe she actually said she was going to go back to the club and put the lock on Paul Krandall?" He threw back his head and laughed as he elbowed Winston in the ribs. "Paul Krandall! You know who he is, right?"

Winston rubbed his side. "The congressman's son? The guy who beat you at tennis?"

Bruce's laughter came to an abrupt stop. "He did *not* beat me at tennis."

"Yes, he did." Winston nodded fiercely, his auburn curls bouncing. "It was in the paper. The paper don't lie, bub."

"He didn't beat me," Bruce insisted. "You just don't know the big picture."

"I *saw* the big picture, Bruce. And Paul was in it with a big ol' trophy." Winston threw up his arms in exasperation. "What was he doing with it? Holding it for you?"

"He cheated," Bruce explained.

"Oh," Winston replied in a tone that clearly implied he didn't believe Bruce.

"I threw the match," Bruce continued, determined to convince him. "Lila made me."

"Uh-huh."

"Winston! I'm telling you—"

Winston held up a finger, interrupting him. "There's a rumor going around about you. You tell

131

me if it's true. You played Paul Krandall for money and he won, so you called the police and tried to have him arrested. But they threatened to arrest *you* for filing a false police report. Did that really happen?"

Bruce's back teeth ground murderously as he remembered just why he and Winston had never been good friends. The guy always seemed to get the wrong end of an idea and hang on for dear life. "Yes," Bruce agreed in mounting frustration. "But that was a different match."

"I see," Winston repeated in a flat, disbelieving tone. "Did Lila make you throw that match too?"

Bruce shook his head and let out a disgusted sigh. Trying to talk to Winston about anything at all was a waste of time. What difference did it make what Denise did or didn't say to Winston? Denise wasn't Lila, and he wasn't Winston. *Thank goodness.* "I'm going inside," Bruce announced, heading for the door.

"Bruce." Winston pulled at his sleeve. "Isn't that Lila's car?"

Bruce turned and saw Lila's car moving south along the street that bordered the campus.

"Yeah," he answered. "I just dropped her off twenty minutes ago. I wonder where she's going?"

"To the country club, perhaps?" Winston suggested.

Bruce snorted in disgust. "Yeah, right. Where did you get *that* idea?"

Chapter Eleven

"You did a great job, Jessica," Chief Wallace said with a smile. "Thanks. And that disguise is wonderful. *I* would never have recognized you."

"You would if you had heard me trying to speak Spanish," Jessica said ruefully. She eased her feet out of her high-heeled pumps and curled her toes. "Wow! I didn't realize how tense I was. My back is killing me." She worked her shoulders around. "Going undercover is rough stuff. You guys are tougher than I thought."

Nick gave her a fond smile. He'd asked Chief Wallace to heap on the extra praise to help Jessica get over the disappointment of letting go of the case, and it seemed to be working—for both of them. "You're pretty tough yourself. That country club life was killing me." He stretched his arms and shook his head, making the slack muscles in his cheek wobble. "My face hurts from smiling."

Jessica laughed, and the sight of her smile made Nick feel better. It had been fun having her along on this gig, but he hoped her desire to play cop had been quenched. He'd meant what he said about Tom and Elizabeth being on a wild-goose chase. But if they weren't, he didn't want Jessica around an explosive situation.

The phone on the chief's desk rang. "Chief Wallace. Yeah?" Over the receiver Nick could hear a man's voice speaking rapidly. The chief reached for a pencil and began scribbling notes. "Yeah? Yeah? Yeah?" he muttered. "All right. I'm going to send some people over."

Nick groaned, praying the call wasn't for him and Jessica. The only place he wanted to be sent with Jessica now was a nice restaurant for a steak and baked potato. He closed his eyes, picturing himself and Jessica sitting in the Old Maple Steak House. The walls were a dark mahogany. The booths were covered in rich red leather. Very private. Lit by a small oil lamp with a flame the color of Jessica's hair. Her *real* hair.

He could picture Jessica sitting next to him, leaning her head on his shoulder. She was blond again. She didn't have that big weird mouth. She was telling him about her day at school. Nobody had gotten robbed. Nobody had gotten hurt. Nobody was dead. Everything in her life was clean and wholesome. And when she talked about her world, it made him feel clean and wholesome too.

"I need you to go to the hospital," Chief Wallace

announced, his deep booming voice shattering Nick's fantasy. "The emergency room. Meet up with Officer Garcia. Jessica, put on your shoes. You're going with Nick."

The romantic spell of the Old Maple Steak House was broken, forcing Nick back reluctantly into the real world of police work.

"I'm bummed," Nick groaned at Jessica.

"Get over it," she commanded, jumping happily to her feet.

Every other syllable was punctuated with a hiss of static on the scanner. "Thirty-five . . . possibly forty males . . . females . . . heat . . . dehydration . . . no fatalities as far as we know."

"Nick! What kind of person would just abandon a transport vehicle with thirty-five or forty people locked inside it?" Jessica gasped.

"A greedy person and a coward," Nick answered grimly. "They're lucky somebody found them."

The police scanner crackled as the report was relayed from unit to unit. Jessica listened intently, trying to decode the messages through the static.

When she saw the lights of the hospital shining through the dark, her stomach tightened and she prepared herself to see something heartbreaking or gruesome. Nick pulled up to the entrance and flashed his badge at the uniformed policeman on duty.

"You Nick Fox?" the policeman asked.

Nick nodded. "And this is my partner, Jessica Wakefield."

In spite of her fears she felt a surge of joy. *This is my partner, Jessica Wakefield.* He'd actually said it. Not, *This is my girlfriend, Jessica; she's helping me out.*

"I'm Peter Garcia." Officer Garcia peered at Jessica through the window and gave her a curt nod of welcome. "Park over there," he instructed. "Then I'll take you upstairs."

Nick rolled up his window and pulled into the space marked Reserved.

"What did I do to rate a promotion?" Jessica asked.

"What do you mean?" Nick asked, arranging his gun so that it was well hidden beneath his leather jacket.

"You said I was your *partner.* Not a girlfriend. Or a trainee. Or something like that."

Nick zipped up his jacket and smiled. "You know, I was thinking on the way over here . . . I mean, don't get me wrong. I'm not saying I like having you along with me. I don't. But you acted like a pro back at the club. You got made. You told me. We left. You handled it like a real policewoman would. You didn't let your ego get in the way of doing the right thing."

Jessica smiled happily, got out of the car, and walked to the entrance with her head held high. Officer Garcia shook their hands and fell into step beside them as they entered the hospital's bright glare.

"We checked with Border Patrol," Officer Garcia

136

began. "Nobody reported seeing the vehicle cross the border, so we don't have a description of the driver or drivers." He shook his head. "I hate these cases. We had one last year where . . ." He trailed off. "Let's just say the people in that emergency room are lucky to be alive. It could have been a lot worse."

"Do you speak Spanish?" Nick asked.

The uniformed policeman nodded.

"Any of the victims able to describe the driver?"

"No. They paid their money to a broker in Monterrey, Mexico. They got in the back of the vehicle at night. Nobody ever got a good look at the driver. The next thing they know, they're abandoned in a steel box with the temperature reaching over one hundred degrees."

Jessica winced, imagining their ordeal.

"Chief Wallace mentioned you were investigating something at the Verona Springs Country Club," Officer Garcia said. "One of the young men keeps repeating something about it."

Nick stopped so quickly, his shoes made a squeak on the floor. He cocked his head and lifted his eyebrows. "You're *kidding*. What is he saying?"

Officer Garcia shrugged. "It was mostly incoherent. The doctor said he couldn't be questioned long, so I waited for you to get here before proceeding any further."

Nick shot a glance at Jessica and lifted his eyebrows. "Interesting twist. This fit in with anything you heard Elizabeth or Tom say?"

Jessica shook her head.

Nick quickened his step. "Let's go see what we can find out. Maybe this is the break we've been hoping for."

They passed a nurses' station and walked through a set of automatic doors. The atmosphere on the other side of those doors was dramatically different. Urgency hung in the air like a thick cloud. Men and women in green scrubs and shower caps hurried around the emergency room. Stethoscopes swayed against their chests as they tugged latex gloves on and off, pushed IVs into place, and conferred with one another.

Fluttering curtains separated the beds. Through them Jessica caught glimpses of feet and heads. She could hear several people moaning. Somewhere a woman sobbed.

Officer Garcia approached a woman making rapid notations on a clipboard. "Doctor, this is Detective Fox and Detective Wakefield. Can we talk to the young man now?"

Detective Wakefield. Jessica liked the sound of that. She felt the corners of her mouth turning up in a pleased smile and forced them back down until her lips formed a professionally grim line. *Don't grin, you idiot! You're in an emergency room! People are hurt!*

The doctor scowled. "He's very weak. Not entirely lucid. If he can't answer your questions, don't press him."

Officer Garcia held up his hand like a Boy Scout taking an oath.

"Five minutes," the doctor told them before hurrying away and disappearing behind a curtain.

Jessica followed Nick and Officer Garcia to the end of the ward. Officer Garcia pulled the curtain aside, and Jessica felt an invisible fist squeeze her heart.

The young man on the bed looked very close to death. His cheeks were sunken. His lips were dried and blistered. Dark circles beneath his eyes emphasized the waxy pallor of his face. "Señor," Officer Garcia said softly. The young man opened his eyes and muttered something in response.

"He says he will tell you what he can," Officer Garcia said.

"Ask him why he wanted to get to the country club," Nick said. "Who was he supposed to see when he got there?"

Officer Garcia translated. In a labored voice the young man answered in Spanish.

"He says he was told that if he could get to the country club, he would be given papers and a job. He was supposed to ask for somebody named Wily Coyote."

"You mean *Wil E. Coyote*? Like the cartoon character?"

"I guess."

"Does he know what Wil E. Coyote looks like?" Nick asked.

Officer Garcia asked the question. The young man shook his head and closed his eyes heavily. Then opened them with a jerk. He reached out and grabbed Jessica's hand, holding it in both of his. In agitated Spanish he seemed to be pleading. Jessica leaned closer, trying to respond but not knowing how. If only she could understand. She felt so helpless! "What is he saying?" Jessica asked.

Officer Garcia gently detached the young man's hand from Jessica's and said something soothing. "He doesn't want to go home. He says he will do anything. Any job. He wants you to help him."

Nick closed his eyes as if he were in pain. "Tell him we'll try," he said. "Tell him we'll do our very best." He took a deep breath and awkwardly patted the young man's arm. *"Adiós. Muchas gracias."*

The young man nodded and laid his head back on his pillow. But he continued to stare at Nick and Jessica as if he were afraid that they would disappear if he closed his eyes.

Officer Garcia held back the curtain, and they moved away from the bed. "I'll tell the doctor we're finished, and I'll meet you outside the ER," he told them.

"Nick," Jessica asked softly as they walked through the automatic doors toward the exit. "What's going to happen to those people?"

"This is one of the best emergency rooms in California," Nick answered. "They'll be OK."

"No, I mean *after.* After they get well. Will they be arrested? They broke the law, right?"

Nick pursed his lips, his shoulders slumping slightly. "Yeah. They did, but they're also crime *victims*. Somebody took advantage of them. Took their money, promised them jobs, and then left them to die."

"Will they go to jail?"

Nick shook his head. "No. They'll just get a free bus ride home."

"It seems so unfair to send them back," she said. "They've already suffered so much, and . . ."

Jessica knew that immigration was a complicated issue. But the young man had asked *her* for help. He had placed his trust in *her*, and now *she* felt responsible. It wasn't a good feeling. She felt overwhelmed. How could she, or she and Nick, possibly solve so many people's problems?

"I think I understand why you don't want to be responsible for me," she said softly. "Being responsible for people, their safety and everything else, is a big . . . *responsibility*."

He put his arm around her and held her close. "People become police officers for all kinds of reasons. But most of them want to do good. They want to help people. Situations like this are tough. It's hard to know how to help and do your job too. That's when you have to remind yourself that you're not the law. You're law *enforcement*. There's a big difference."

"I do want to help," Jessica murmured into his shoulder. "I just wish I knew how."

"The best way we can help our friend up there is to find out who did this—and keep them from doing it to anybody else," Nick said, resting his chin on the top of her head.

The doors behind them opened, and Nick released her when Officer Garcia appeared. Jessica felt the reluctance in his arms. But she knew that when he was on the job—when *they* were on the job—it was important to be as professional as possible.

"Where is the vehicle?" Nick asked him, reaching into his back pocket to remove a notebook. "I want to go out and take a look at it."

"It's still sitting where it was found. Two kids spotted it and called in the report. They thought maybe it was stolen. They didn't know anybody was in it."

"What kind of vehicle is it?"

"It's a red cargo van—" Officer Garcia began.

Jessica let out a small scream. "A red cargo van! Nick! I saw a red cargo van this morning. Remember?"

"There are cargo vans all over the road," Nick said.

"Yeah. But how many of them are red? And how many have a missing mud flap?"

"Was the van missing a mud flap?" Nick asked Officer Garcia.

"I don't know."

Nick smiled slowly at Jessica. "Let's check it out. If you're right, Perdita, you just might wind up with the biggest collar of the year."

Jessica's fatigue and frustration vanished, and she giggled. "I was thinking that all I wanted right now was a hot bath. But a hot tip is *way* more refreshing."

Chapter
Twelve

How could anybody leave thirty-five to forty people in a transport vehicle to die? Tom wondered, boggled by what he was hearing over the scanner.

Carlos was warning me, he decided as he changed lanes and headed for the exit ramp. *He knew something was going down and I was getting too close.*

Tom clenched his teeth. Anybody callous and cold-blooded enough to leave people to die of heat and thirst would have no compunction about killing Tom if he got in the way. Carlos either.

Carlos was a good guy. He didn't deserve to be in the position of trying to protect people on his staff from . . .

Who?

Paul?

Impossible, Tom's brain insisted. Paul was a shake-down artist and a pea brain. According to the information on the scanner, the vehicle was new and the plates were clean. That would have taken capital and an ongoing stream of money coming in to finance the operation.

Whoever brought those people across the border into California was a big operator and probably did it on a regular basis—brought them in and dropped them off somewhere in the area.

He moved over one more lane. Another car came up the ramp to his right. Out of the right-hand mirror Tom caught a glimpse of the driver. Nick Fox!

"Thanks, Nick." Tom chuckled, turning off his blinker. "You just saved me a trip to the hospital. I'm sure they told you more than they would have told me!"

Nick's car was moving faster than traffic, but he wasn't speeding. That was good. As long as he didn't stick that cherry on the top and turn on the siren, Tom could shadow them and see where this strange story was going. He smiled. *Touché, Elizabeth Wakefield.*

"Slow down. Slow down," Scott cautioned.

Elizabeth tapped the brake pedal of the big gray Econoline van. It had felt a little unwieldy at first, but she took to it like a duck to water. "Did he see us?"

Scott's blue eyes watched Tom's taillights. "No," he said. "I don't think so. But let this Mazda on the right get in front of us. If Tom looks in his rearview, he'll know he's being followed. We've been behind him for a long time."

Elizabeth smiled. "Even if he spots me, he can't lose me. This ain't my first time at the rodeo, you know."

Scott laughed. "Now was I right, or was I right? I knew we might want to follow Tom. And he would have spotted my car behind him in a New York minute."

Elizabeth lifted her hand and waited for Scott to smack it. "You were right. This van was a master stroke." She smiled, remembering the way they had left the reception, walked right past Scott's conspicuous yellow convertible, and gotten inside the van, where they could watch the parking lot from behind the dark windows.

"It's strange that Tom didn't leave with Dana," Scott commented. "That tells me he's got business he doesn't want her to know about."

Elizabeth bit her lip in frustration. "Yeah. But what? So far he's stopped at his dorm and the station. Nothing to write about there."

"*Now* where's he going?" Scott murmured as they followed Tom around a large interchange.

"It looks like he's heading back to the club," Elizabeth said.

"Maybe he forgot something."

Like Dana? Elizabeth wondered. "If Tom doesn't lead us to the story," she said, trying to think ahead, "I think we should go back to the club tomorrow and talk to the golf pro." Her hands tightened on the wheel, steering the van around a slow-moving sedan. "We'll talk to the manager again too. And his secretary. When I talked to them before, I didn't know what questions to ask."

She sped up a little, unwilling to let too much distance develop between her and Tom.

A lump rose in her throat. The distance between her and Tom was wider than the Pacific. Not long ago the thought of following Tom would have horrified her. *And I accused him of low tactics!* she berated herself. This one was pretty low too. Tears began to sting her eyes. She tried to sniff quietly so Scott wouldn't hear.

But Scott didn't miss much.

"Here." He handed her a tissue.

Elizabeth took it and dabbed at her nose, blinking the teary blur from her eyes. "I'm sorry," she managed to squeak.

He reached over and steadied the wheel while she blew her nose. "I'm the one who should be apologizing. I know how much you cared about Tom. This is probably hard."

She nodded, stuffed the wadded tissue into her pocket, and put her hands back on the wheel. She looked over her left shoulder. A blue Nissan whizzed past, weaving in and out of traffic. The Nissan obscured Tom's car for a moment, then changed lanes.

When it did, Tom's car was gone! "Where'd he go?" Elizabeth cried.

Scott let out a little noise of surprise and alarm. Elizabeth hit the pedal and pressed ahead of the two moving vans coming up the entrance ramp. "Do you see him?" she asked frantically, scared to death Tom had figured out that the gray van behind him was commandeered by none other than her.

"He's over there. In the *left* lane!" Scott looked over the seat. "Go . . . go . . . go . . ."

She had a blind spot, but she trusted Scott and pounded the pedal while pulling the wheel to the left. As soon as she was in the proper lane a car appeared in her rearview mirror, almost on her bumper. She had cut right in front of it with only inches to spare. The car beeped indignantly before dropping back. *He's not going back for Dana after all,* Elizabeth realized, wishing she didn't care one way or the other. But she did, and she couldn't help feeling happy that whatever Tom was up to, his plans didn't include Dana.

Tom was right in front of them now. She could see the back of his head. The overhead lights on the freeway glared down over the interchange so brightly that Elizabeth could see Tom's eyes in his rearview mirror. They were staring right into hers. She gasped and managed to keep herself from slamming on the brakes.

He can't see me, she realized, her heart racing. The glass on the van was so dark, there was no way Tom could see who was driving. *He's looking right at me, and he doesn't see me.*

It was an incredibly painful thought.

"If this is Bruce, I'm having dinner with Paul. And by the way, why are you calling me when I told you not to?"

Bruce slammed down the phone and threw himself on his bed. Lila Fowler was without a doubt the most disloyal and untrustworthy girlfriend he had ever had. And that was no small feat. He punched his pillow and pushed the newspapers onto the floor. How could Lila not see what a phony Paul Krandall was? How phony they *all* were?

Bruce turned moodily, and his left eye bulged when he saw Paul Krandall grinning up at him from the pile of papers on the rug. What will Paul do next? the headline screamed obnoxiously.

"How about fifteen to twenty at the nearest correctional facility," Bruce muttered under his breath. He rolled off the bed and paced, getting angrier and angrier.

Lila had made him look like a bad tennis player and a bad sport. Lila had exposed him to ridicule. Lila had used him to get into the Verona Springs Country Club and then discarded him like a used tissue. And she'd done it to make points with a bunch of classless morons.

Bruce crumpled up the newspaper and threw it in the wastebasket. "What will *Bruce* do next?" he snarled, picking up his silver-framed photo of Lila. An evil chuckle escaped his lips as his mind began formulating a diabolical plan of action. "I'll tell you this much, Li." He slammed down the picture and reached for his keys. "It ain't gonna be pretty."

Chapter
Thirteen

"Pull over at the fence under the billboard just before you get to Reservoir Road." Jessica read the directions from Nick's notebook. She glanced up and pointed. "There, I guess."

Nick cruised off the exit that led to the interchange and pulled onto the shoulder of the road beneath a blank billboard.

A stream of cars passed them by. Some turned and took the road that led back to town. Some took the road that led to the country club and surrounding suburbs. Some continued on toward Los Angeles. None turned onto Reservoir Road, a twisting, turning four-mile road with no lights. Some of her Theta sisters jogged there, but always in the daytime. Never at night.

Jessica looked up curiously as a gray van with dark windows passed them slowly. *Is that van following us?* she wondered. *Guess not,* she decided when it continued on, disappearing into the night.

Nick waited until all the cars were out of sight before turning off the engine and cutting the lights. "Let's go. Two miles south, right?"

Jessica got out and looked around. A rickety barbed wire fence ran along the highway. She cringed at the tangle of brush and trees that lay behind it. "Yikes! I'll need to get some boots out of the trunk. I can't walk through that in these platforms. I mean, they're open toed."

Nick opened the trunk, and Jessica quickly rifled through her suitcase, searching for her high-top sneakers. She pulled off her pumps and put the sneakers on over her stockings while Nick locked up the car.

"Ready to frolic in the pampas, Perdita?" Nick teased, holding out his hand.

She took it and held it tightly. "I'm ready, but not to frolic. I'm ready to kick butt!"

Nick laughed and slammed the trunk shut with his free hand. "Then let's take a hike." He ducked down under the broken barbed wire and held it for Jessica. She stooped gracefully underneath it.

Under normal circumstances she would balk at the suggestion of a two-mile walk. But being out in the countryside with Nick on police business put a spring in her step as she marched beside him.

The tall grass brushed around Jessica's ankles and shins. She could feel the burred leaf edges snagging the fragile rayon of her dress. *It'll be ruined,* she worried. *So what? Perdita's cover is blown. I won't be needing this disguise again.*

Behind them Jessica heard the yawn of engines moving through the interchange. The noise grew fainter as they got farther from the road. She wasn't scared, though. The moon hung overhead like a lamp, providing a reassuring light.

"You're always trying to convince me that undercover work is dull. Ha! I *knew* it was romantic," she teased. "You just didn't want me to know because then I'd want to come with you every time."

"*This is* romantic," he agreed. He pulled her to a stop and wrapped his arms around her waist. She turned her face up, and they kissed for a long, long time. Nick's stubble was rough, but its scrape and tickle as he nuzzled her neck made her feel as if she were slowly melting.

The sense of urgency she had felt when they left the hospital faded. The case, the club, and the clues all swirled away as his hands moved up and down her back. "I never thought I'd feel this way about a partner," he breathed.

Jessica tightened her arms around him. "Does that mean you've decided you don't need to keep your personal and professional lives separate?" she whispered.

He laughed. "Did I say that?"

"Mm-hmmm. Today, as a matter of fact."

"No," he said, loosening his grasp around her waist until she swayed in his embrace. "That was Chip. Not me."

"Whatever happened to that Chip guy?"

Nick shrugged. "He was too uptight. He got on my nerves. I told him you weren't interested. I think he's dating Bunny now."

Jessica threw back her head and laughed. "My goodness, Detective Fox. What's gotten into you? I haven't seen you in this kind of mood for a long time."

He pulled her against his chest and rubbed his cheek against hers. "Hospitals and police stations remind me that life is short. Moonlight and tall grass remind me that life is good."

She could feel him unwinding. Relaxing in her arms. He let out a long sigh, and she ran her hand through his short but still shaggy hair.

Suddenly Jessica felt the muscles in Nick's back bunch. He abruptly lifted his head. "Did you hear that?"

"No. What?"

Nick stood perfectly still for a moment. "I thought I heard something."

"Some*thing*? Or some*body*?" she asked, a shiver of fear hurrying down her arms.

"Lila, I think the college vote is going to be very important. I *know* my constituents. I'm on *their* side. This is *their* year. Yes. The student media is *the single biggest* influence *in* the nation right *now*, and . . ."

Lila tried to tune out Congressman Krandall's voice so she could concentrate on Paul. She smiled at him, and he smiled back—a smile of deep and intimate understanding.

Paul and his father had been waiting for her in the ballroom when she arrived. Carlos, the headwaiter, had shown them to a table on the patio where some of Congressman Krandall's people were waiting. The silver trophy full of discreetly folded checks sat on the table in conspicuous view. Lila had dropped a second contribution in the cup before sitting down.

Lila looked around the pool area. She could see Anderson and Pepper at a nearby table. She also spotted several other VIPs watching their table with interest. "Where is Bunny?" she asked with a sly smile. She knew full well that Paul had given Bunny the brush. Knowing the way the VIP Circle worked, everybody else probably knew it too.

Paul's hand slid across the white enamel surface of the table, and he moved his finger over her wrist. "She didn't feel good, so she went home."

Lila lifted her forefinger and intertwined it in Paul's. "What a shame." She couldn't help peeping over to see Pepper's reaction. She'd leaned her head toward Anderson's and was whispering wildly.

A momentary pang of guilt passed through Lila's chest. Maybe she shouldn't have dumped Bruce so unceremoniously. But when she remembered how hard he had worked to humiliate her, she shoved it aside. The Bruce Era was over.

"Well, well, well!" a familiar voice exclaimed. Paul jumped.

Lila looked up, startled. "Bruce!" she squeaked.

Bruce stood at the foot of the table next to Congressman Krandall with the ugliest look on his face she had ever seen. He let out a snort of disgust and lifted a sneering lip to reveal a canine tooth. He put his hands on his hips and surveyed the group.

"Sit down, young man. Sit down," Congressman Krandall boomed, standing up and smiling as if Bruce's arrival was some kind of unexpected but delightful surprise.

Lila rolled her eyes. Congressman Krandall was nice, but he was *so* clueless. *I sure do hope he's not negotiating missile treaties or anything like that. If so, we're doomed!*

"No, thanks. I'm not sitting down," Bruce snapped. "And I'm not lying down either. This club is part of a very dirty business." He raised his voice and looked around the patio, addressing his remarks to the group at large.

Table by table, the patio became quiet.

Carlos, who had been pouring water behind Paul, jumped, splashing a little water on Paul's plate. Lila watched him unobtrusively reach for a napkin to wipe it up. But as he worked, his eyes were glued to Bruce.

"What do you mean?" Congressman Krandall demanded.

"Extortion! Blackmail! That's what I mean."

Paul dropped his fork. It clattered to the ground.

"Inviting people here so you could lean on

154

them to make a big contribution to your campaign. And stealing their girlfriends if they don't toe the line."

Carlos smiled, and his shoulders shook with silent laughter as he moved on with the water pitcher.

Trust Bruce to make a total fool of himself! Lila thought angrily. *Even the help is laughing at him.*

"Now see here," one of the congressman's people began.

"No!" Bruce shouted. "*You* see here!" He grabbed the trophy and turned it over. The checks fell out and fluttered across the table and the pea-graveled patio. Bruce flicked his nail against the trophy. It made a flat, tinny sound. "I thought so," he said scornfully. "Plated. Phony. Just like the Verona Springs VIPs."

Anderson stood up. "Listen here, Patman . . ."

"That's Paaahhhtman to you," Bruce mocked. "Talk like a real person, you . . . you . . . you *pretentious little snipe!*"

Anderson sat down, squelched. Pepper hissed at him to *do* something, but Anderson just looked on with a scowl.

Lila sat back in her seat, torn between fury and delight. On the one hand, Bruce seemed to be absolutely determined to get her thrown out of the country club. On the other hand, it was kind of exciting being able to inspire that much rage in a man.

She looked across the table at Paul, waiting for him to stand up to Bruce. Wow! *The girls at the sorority house will talk about this for years to come,* she thought happily. *This night will go down in Theta history as the night Bruce Patman and Paul Krandall fought over Lila Fowler at the Verona Springs Country Club.*

She looked around, wondering if there were any gossip columnists in the crowd. She made a mental note to look for her name in the next edition of *Scene*.

Unfortunately Paul stayed rooted in his chair and shot a dark look toward the headwaiter. "Carlos!" he prompted.

Carlos obediently stepped forward. "I'm afraid I'm going to have to ask you to leave," he said politely but firmly.

Lila's mouth fell open. Was Paul really going to make the headwaiter deal with Bruce?

She looked over at Congressman Krandall and his people.

Nobody moved.

Carlos put the water pitcher down and placed his hand on Bruce's arm. "Sir . . ."

Bruce yanked his arm away and tucked the trophy underneath it. "I'm leaving," he announced, drawing himself up to his full height.

"Where are you taking that trophy?" Paul demanded.

"I'm going to throw it in the Verona Springs Reservoir," Bruce shouted. "You can dive for it at your next VIP get-together." Bruce broke into a run. Everyone on the patio jumped to their feet and surged toward the door behind him.

Lila stepped back, trying to see what was happening over the headwaiter's head. One step. Two steps. And then suddenly she felt as if she had stepped off the edge of the earth. She opened her mouth to scream, but before she could make a sound, the cold water of the swimming pool closed over her head.

"Keep moving," Nick whispered. "And keep your eyes open. We may not be alone out here."

She nodded and tried to step carefully through the thicket. Nick walked ahead of her, shoving low-hanging branches aside and pointing out treacherous roots.

A cloud moved in front of the moon. It was as if someone had extinguished the light. "Nick!" she cried out involuntarily.

"I'm here," he answered in a low tone. A rustle of wings in the tree made them both jump. She clutched his sleeve. "It's a bird," he soothed.

They walked on in silence. Their feet made a shushing, crunching sound in the brush. Every once in a while Nick would come to a sudden stop and listen in case someone else was shushing and crunching through the woods behind them.

Jessica thought she heard something, but it was impossible to be sure. It might have been the blood throbbing through her ears. The farther into the thicket they walked, the more nervous she became. Her heart hammered inside her chest. Was Nick as frightened as she? She didn't dare ask him. What if he said yes?

Nick unzipped his jacket, and Jessica swallowed nervously. *Well, there's your answer,* she told herself. She knew why he had opened his jacket. So he would be able to reach his gun if he needed it.

He pushed aside a branch, and they stepped into a clearing. A huge shadow loomed in the center. It was hard to see at first, but then the large shadow took shape. It was the cargo van.

Jessica cried out and stumbled forward, forgetting her fear for a moment. She ran around the back of the vehicle. "Nick! It *is* the van I saw this morning. It's missing a mud flap."

Nick came around and dropped down on one knee to examine the wheel. "You're right. Look at th—" Without any warning at all he reached up, grabbed Jessica's hand, and yanked her to the ground.

Before she even had time to scream, Nick was in motion. He rolled over her, and she could feel his arm thrusting into his jacket. A second and a half later he was lying between her and the thicket. Prone, on his stomach, with his gun pointed toward the tree line. "Freeze!" he shouted.

Tom's heart jumped out of his chest and into his mouth. He'd never seen anything happen so fast in his life. One second Nick was peering under a van, and the next he was aiming the barrel of a wicked-looking pistol at Tom's chest.

"Come out with your hands up," Nick bellowed.

Tom was so surprised, he couldn't react. But the ominous click of Nick's gun registered in his belly and propelled him into action. He lifted his hands. "Don't shoot! Please!"

"Come out of there!" Nick shouted.

Tom moved out of the woods and into the clearing as slowly and carefully as possible. He didn't want to do anything that Nick might interpret as a threat. "It's me, Tom Watts."

Jessica lifted her head and blinked. "Tom? What are you doing out here?"

Nick climbed to his feet, still holding his gun on Tom. "Yeah. What *are* you doing out here?" he asked in a heavy, accusatory tone. "Are you part of this *slave trade?*" He gestured toward the van.

Tom shook his head. "No! No way! Not in a million years."

"Then what are you doing here?" Nick eyed him with suspicion.

"I followed you," Tom admitted, glad that the darkness would hide his red face.

"Followed us from where?" Nick asked.

"From the hospital. I was on my way there to check out the story about the people found in the transport vehicle. When I saw you get on the freeway, I decided to follow."

"Those people at the hospital are strictly police business," Nick said slowly. "If you're not part of this operation, how did you know they were there?" He slowly approached Tom and began to pat his pockets, searching for a weapon.

Jessica got to her feet, brushing leaves and twigs from her clothes and hair.

Once again Tom was grateful for the dark. It hid his telltale blush. "Tell him I'm not a criminal, Jessica." Tom looked over at her for support. "Please."

But Jessica crossed her arms and cocked her hip. "That's not how it works," she said dryly, imitating the tone he had used when he said the same thing to her in the kitchen.

He groaned. "All right," he admitted. "I knew what happened because I heard the report. I have a scanner. I'd rather you think I'm a snoop than a slave trader."

Nick backed away. "What do you mean you have a scanner? That's illegal."

Tom nodded. "Yeah. I know. But sometimes it's a legitimate news-gathering—"

"Shut up!" Nick thrust his gun angrily back into its holster and ran his hands through his hair in frustration. "What is it with you reporters? Huh? What makes you think your Mickey Mouse newspaper and TV station have any right at all to jeopardize a police investigation? I'm . . . I'm through with all of you."

Nick removed a pair of handcuffs from his jacket and jerked Tom's arms behind his back. "I've had it. This is the last straw. I'm running you in and booking you."

"What!" Tom yelped. "Come *on*. You're not serious." Tom did his best not to struggle while Nick fastened the steel cuffs behind his back.

"I *am* serious. I just don't know how else to make my point."

"I'm not trying jeopardize your investigation," Tom insisted. "Maybe I can help you. I think I know what's going on and who's behind it."

"Oh yeah?" Nick said. "Enlighten me."

"Take the cuffs off first," Tom said.

"Are you actually trying to negotiate with me, you little sneak?" Nick exploded. "After what you did? Do you have *any idea* how *dangerous* it is to sneak up on a police officer? Do you? You could have gotten yourself killed." Nick turned and began angrily kicking the wheel of the cargo van.

"Why are you kicking the van?" Jessica cried.

"Because it's illegal to kick *him*," Nick yelled, kicking the wheel yet again.

"Stop doing that," Jessica begged. "You're wasting time."

"It makes me feel better," Nick shouted.

Jessica threw up her hands. "You have *such* a double standard. If I acted that way, you would tell me to stop being so childish. You're always telling me to stay cool and stay calm."

Nick stopped kicking the tire. "Jessica, sometimes I really get tired of having to tell you my reasons for every single . . ."

Tom rolled his eyes. If Jessica and Nick wanted to have a lovers' quarrel, they could have it on their own time. "Excuse me," he said, interrupting their argument. "Could we resolve this handcuff matter? I really—" He broke off when he heard a noise in the bushes.

161

Nick heard it too. He stopped in midkick.

Jessica's eyes grew large with fright, and for one split second they all stood motionless.

Then Tom's terror synapse fired, and Nick screamed, "Get down!" Tom tried to react, but he just couldn't make his body move fast enough. *We're going to die,* he thought as Nick dove toward him, knocking him backward.

"Not again!" Jessica wailed as Nick pulled her to the ground beside him and cocked his gun.

"Freeze!" Nick bellowed.

Tom stared up at the sky, wondering if this was his last look at the Big Dipper.

Chapter Fourteen

"Yikes!" Elizabeth shrieked when she saw the gun pointing straight at her. She went numb with shock all the way to her fingertips.

Scott immediately stepped in front of her and raised his arms. "Don't shoot!" he said in a clear, calm voice. He started forward. Elizabeth followed him into the clearing on shaking legs.

The scene was surreal. Tom Watts lay on his back and side with his hands cuffed behind him. Jessica lay next to him in a heap on the ground. And Nick was poised with his gun, ready to protect them both.

"Elizabeth!" Jessica exclaimed.

Tom let out a groan of relief. "Thank goodness. I thought we were dead."

Elizabeth's eyes settled on the cargo van. *Now what have we here,* she thought, curiosity beginning to replace fear.

Nick stood up. His nostrils flared as he took long

and noisy breaths. "I don't believe this! What are you two doing here? Are you people *trying* to drive me nuts? Did you *plan* this?"

"Sorry we startled you," Scott said, his voice steady.

How does Scott do it? Elizabeth marveled. *Does anything rattle him?* Elizabeth's knees were knocking, and her voice was still stuck in her chest somewhere. But Scott was cool as a cucumber.

"*Startled?*" Nick repeated incredulously. "*Startled?* I'm not *startled!* I'm *terrified!* Who's going to come popping out of the woods next? Big Foot? The Great Pumpkin? Elvis? Tell me, 'cause I really wanna know!"

"I hope not," Elizabeth squeaked, meaning it. "We didn't see or hear anything—besides you guys."

"How did you two get here?" Nick demanded.

"We followed Tom," Scott explained. "We didn't know *he* was following *you* till we got here."

"What?" Tom let out an outraged growl from the ground. "You couldn't have followed me!"

"Why not?" Elizabeth asked.

"I'd *know* if someone were following me."

Scott lifted his lip in a sneer. "In your dreams, *Mr. Bond.*" He looked at Nick. "May I put my hands down now?"

"No!" Nick exploded. "Keep your hands where I can see them. That way you can't get into any trouble."

Elizabeth didn't blame Nick for being angry. But

she wished he'd quit yelling and waving his arms around. It made him look like a TV cop. All macho bluster. And right now she really wanted to talk about that cargo van.

Nick walked over to her and thrust his face into hers. "Let's start with you. From the beginning. What do you know?"

"I don't *know* anything," Elizabeth hedged. It was true, after all. She didn't have any hard evidence. All she had was a theory.

"OK," he said, clearly catching on. "Let's talk about what you *suspect*."

Elizabeth stared stonily ahead, determined not to answer.

"Ever been in jail?" Nick asked conversationally.

"No," Elizabeth answered.

"Then it will be a new experience for you," Nick said in a sticky sweet voice. "For all of you. You're under arrest."

"On what charge?" Tom shouted.

"I'll think of something," Nick bellowed.

"*Ni*-ick!" Jessica scolded. "Stop being such a bully."

Elizabeth glanced down at Tom. His eyes met hers, and Elizabeth remembered their intense stare in the rearview mirror. She looked away, worried that she might burst into tears again.

Nick took some deep breaths and dropped his gun. "OK. OK. This isn't going to get us anywhere." He walked over to Tom, helped him to

his feet, and dusted him off. "Let's all start over."
He removed the handcuffs. "I'm sorry I lost my
temper. What can I say?" He laughed dryly. "I'm
just feeling a little moody this evening." Nick
stuffed the key down into the front pocket of his
jeans. "You're all to be commended on your dili-
gent pursuit of the truth," he said in a conde-
scending tone. "So let's hear it. What have you
whiz kids come up with? Tom? Why don't you
share your wisdom with the group."

Tom shifted on his feet. "I'd like to hear what
Elizabeth has to say first."

Elizabeth let out a little bark of indignation. "I
thought you stopped playing that game!"

"I want *everybody* to stop playing games," Nick
said, turning toward her. "Now speak up."

Elizabeth squared her shoulders, determined
not to be bullied by Nick or Tom or anybody else.
"Let's talk about that cargo van first." She braced
herself for another explosion of temper, but before
Nick could react, Jessica gasped.

"Nick," Jessica hissed. "I think somebody's coming." She ran over to the back of the cargo van.

"Everybody get down," Nick instructed.

"No," Jessica whispered. "You can't protect
everybody by yourself. Get in the van. Hide." She
pulled open the doors. "Hurry."

"She's right," Nick said. "Go on. Everybody
get in." He put his hand on Elizabeth's arm and
pushed her in Jessica's direction. Elizabeth
jumped into the back of the van. Behind her came

Scott, Tom, and Nick. Nick turned and reached out to pull Jessica in, but instead of allowing him to lift her up, Jessica pulled away.

"Jessica!" Elizabeth protested.

"What are you doing?" Nick cried.

Elizabeth started forward at the same time Nick did. But before they could jump out, Jessica closed the door on their faces with a slam.

Nick backed up and examined the door, trying to figure out if there were some way to open it from the inside. What the heck was Jessica up to now?

"Here. I've got a flashlight." Tom produced a small black flashlight and shone a beam of light at the doors.

Scott came over and ran his hand along the seam.

"Don't you think if it opened from the inside, those poor people would have let themselves out?" Jessica hollered. "You're locked in."

Nick whirled around and saw part of Jessica's face behind a tiny grate in the front of the cargo van. "What's going on? Is somebody out there or not?"

"Not!" Jessica answered. "I tricked you guys. I thought a little togetherness might help you figure out how to communicate."

"Jessica," Nick sputtered. "This is really cute, but—"

"You guys are going to learn to work together, and you're not coming out until you do," Jessica said.

167

The group crowded up to the grate.

"Jessica!" Elizabeth pleaded. "Open the door. This is ridiculous."

"Open the door," Scott ordered coolly. "Or—"

"Or what?" Jessica asked. "What are you going to do? You're completely at my mercy. You're locked in. Nobody can hear you shout for help. If I walk off and leave you here, you'll die. I'm giving you guys a very small taste of what those people went through."

Nick's heart sank. Just when he was beginning to hope Jessica had started to think like a professional, she had to go and pull another kooky stunt. "Figures," he said. "I'm a sap."

"You're basically entombed," Jessica continued.

Elizabeth's heart began to thud, and she couldn't catch her breath. Maybe she was claustrophobic without realizing it. She moved her face closer to the grate so that the small stream of cool night air could reach her face. "You've made your point. Let us out," she begged.

"If you guys want out, you'll put your egos aside and work together," Jessica responded.

"Why are you doing this?" Tom said.

"Because I promised somebody I would help him," Jessica answered quietly. "And this is the only solution I could think of." With that she closed the grate.

The current of air came to an abrupt stop.

Elizabeth gulped and tried to catch her breath. It was hard. It had been an emotional roller coaster of a day, and all her feelings and anxieties suddenly felt like a five–hundred–pound weight on her chest. She stumbled back from the grate and began to pant.

"She's hyperventilating!" Scott's calm voice lost a fraction of its composure. "Try to breath rhythmically," he instructed. "Do either of you guys have a paper bag?"

It was such a ridiculous question, Elizabeth forgot the pressure on her chest and began to laugh. The thought of standing here breathing into a bag was just . . . *hilarious*.

The guys watched her laugh with expressions of concern.

"She's hysterical," Nick said.

Elizabeth shook her head. "No . . . I'm . . . not," she managed to say. "It's just . . . funny! A *paper bag!*" she repeated, laughing so hard she thought her sides might split.

Tom began to giggle and pat his pockets, as if he were trying to locate something. "Gosh darn it. I guess I left my paper bag at home."

Nick's wrathful expression gave way to a smile. He leaned back against the wall and slid to the floor, laughing. Scott crossed his arms and snickered.

Elizabeth opened the collar of her blouse and lifted her long hair off the back of her neck. She took a few moments to pull herself together before speaking. "I think Jessica's right. We've all lost our perspective. This competition has gone too far. I'm willing to tell you what we've found out so far. But I still don't know what it means."

Elizabeth took a deep breath and launched into her side of the story. She told them about taking the envelope of mail from the club office and finding the postcard informing Manoel Coimbra that his voting location had changed. She told them that the county records showed that Manoel Coimbra was not a nineteen-year-old resident alien but a deceased naturalized citizen from Brazil.

"So whoever was working at the club using Manoel Coimbra's name and social security number," she concluded, "was not really Manoel Coimbra."

Nick's forehead furrowed thoughtfully. "The graveyard vote's been around for a long time. But politicians aren't the only people who find deceased voters useful. People in the business of selling phony IDs and working papers tend to use social security numbers and voter registration information. Then they sell them to illegal immigrants desperate to find work. People easily exploited by other people willing to pack them into vans and haul them like cattle," he added significantly.

"And then exploited again by people who extort money from them." Tom squatted down on his heels. "People like Paul Krandall."

"Are you talking about that big wad of cash Paul had in the parking lot?" Elizabeth asked.

Tom nodded. "That money was collected from

the Latino club employees. Supposedly as a wedding gift for somebody who used to work there."

"How do you know that?" Elizabeth asked.

"Because I contributed. I wrote *buena suerte* on a ten-dollar bill and gave it to . . . one of the employees. When Paul pulled out that wad of cash, I saw that same ten-dollar bill. I know it was that bill because I saw my own handwriting on it."

Elizabeth blew out her breath. "Wow! I'd say that nails Paul dead solid perfect."

"Not necessarily," Scott interjected. "Let's say the guy who collected the money had a bunch of tens, a bunch of fives, and a bunch of ones. A great big wad of money. He doesn't want to carry it around all day. He doesn't want to leave it in his locker. So he asks whoever is at the cash register to hold on to it. When he picks it up, he asks for fifties. Or even twenties. And he leaves the smaller bills in the cash drawer. Once a bill's in the cash drawer, it could wind up anywhere. In your pocket. Mine. Paul Krandall's."

"No," Elizabeth argued. "That's improbable because it's a private club. Nobody uses cash at a private club. They sign for everything, and it's charged to an account."

Tom nodded. "That's true. I never saw any cash around the club. So there was no way it would circulate." He hitched up the knees of his jeans and sat on the floor. "So this guy Coimbra—not the real Coimbra, the fake one. Where is he now?"

Elizabeth shook her head. "I don't know where he is or where the gardener is. But there's more. . . ."

For once I'm glad I'm not a real policewoman. Jessica giggled. A real policewoman wouldn't have been able to ignore police procedure and take matters into her own hands the way Jessica had.

She glanced at her watch. *All right, folks. You've been in there a long time. Let's see how you're doing.* Jessica turned and opened the partition between the cab and the van. But just as she was reaching for the little grate somebody grabbed her from behind.

Terrified out of her wits, Jessica flailed and struggled. She tried to scream, but a hand closed over her mouth and nose and pressed, almost cutting off all her air. Jessica kicked wildly as the pressure in her lungs mounted. Her fingers clawed at the hand over her mouth, and she tried to bite. But the viselike hand was encased in a thick glove. Jessica dug with her fingernails and felt them bend and break like paper.

Her attacker swung her out of the cab and slammed her onto the ground, facedown, removing his hand from her mouth. "If you make one sound, I'll kill you," he whispered. "Understand?"

Jessica's breath came in ragged and shallow gasps and her chest felt ready to explode.

"Understand?" he repeated roughly.

Trembling, Jessica nodded slightly. *Nick! Nick!*

Where are you? she thought, then realized that he was locked in the transport, even more helpless than she.

Her attacker pulled a sack down over her head. The cloth was rough and hot.

"Get up."

Jessica struggled to her feet, trying to place the voice. It was familiar. Very familiar. *Paul Krandall!* she realized with a shock so great, she fell to the ground.

A rough hand closed over her upper arm and yanked her to a standing position. "Stand *up!*" he ordered. "Hold out your hands."

Jessica hesitated for only a moment, then quickly held them out. He tied her wrists together with tight, jerky motions. Then he grabbed her arm and pulled her several steps. Was he going to kill her? Where were they going?

Jessica began to shudder from head to toe. Then she heard the door of the cab open. He picked her up and shoved her inside on the floor. "Stay down there," he ordered, putting his hand on her head and shoving it beneath the dashboard. "And be quiet."

The door closed, and Jessica heard him walk away, his heavy boots crushing the grass and weeds. She whimpered slightly. There was no way anyone could hear anything in the van. They had no idea they were in danger. No idea that *she* was in danger. And even if they *did* know, the two people that Jessica could depend on to rescue her were helpless now to help her—or themselves.

Tears of fear and shame rolled down her cheeks. "It's my fault," she shuddered in a whisper. "My fault for being childish and impulsive!" The thought was so horrifying, she could hardly bear it. An involuntary moan escaped her lips as grief and remorse overwhelmed her.

She pictured Nick. The way he always looked at her with wonder and amusement dancing in his jade green eyes. Could he ever look at her again with anything but contempt? Would he ever have the chance?

Not if she didn't do something.

Why am I lying here on the floor? she scolded herself. She might not be able to rescue them, but she had a responsibility to at least try. Buoyed with determination, she tried to leap to her feet.

Her head hit the dashboard with a sickening thump. A shower of glaring sparks briefly illuminated the dark behind her eyes.

Then everything went black.

". . . So Dwayne was murdered because he noticed that the spelling of Manoel's name, with an *o* instead of a *u*, was Portuguese and not Spanish," Elizabeth explained. "In Mexico the name would typically be given the Spanish spelling."

Tom frowned, trying to follow the thread of her reasoning. "So what? I don't get it."

"I get it," Nick said, throwing Elizabeth a smile and an admiring glance. "Wow! That's first-class work, Elizabeth."

174

Elizabeth felt a flush of pleasure. She knew that Nick didn't hand out compliments if he didn't mean them.

"Manoel Coimbra had said he was from Mexico. But because of the spelling Dwayne realized Manoel was using a phony name and was probably an illegal immigrant," Nick explained to Tom. "Manoel was afraid Dwayne might turn him in or blackmail him."

Tom expelled his breath. "Nowwww I see. So Coimbra murdered Dwayne and planted the stuff on Phillips." This time *Tom* threw Elizabeth a look of admiration.

"Not necessarily," she said. "It's also possible that whoever murdered Dwayne and framed Phillips murdered Coimbra too. And that would be the person running this operation."

In spite of the dark, the heat, and the discomfort Elizabeth felt more confident and focused than she had in days—largely because she was able to talk to Tom. He recharged and stimulated her brain in a way that Scott didn't.

"Does the name Wil E. Coyote mean anything to anybody here?" Nick asked.

"It's a cartoon character," Tom said. "In the old Road Runner cartoons."

"A coyote is also somebody who smuggles in immigrants," Nick explained. "One of the people at the hospital was told to go to the country club and ask for Wil E. Coyote. He would see that he got working papers and a job."

"Paul must be Wil E. Coyote," Scott suggested.

"It's exactly the kind of dumb pun he'd come up with."

Nick shook his head. "I don't think so. He's not smart enough to put this together by himself. He's got a partner."

Elizabeth and Tom looked at each other. "Congressman Krandall!" they both said at once.

"It makes perfect sense," Elizabeth said. "Congressman Krandall's got the voting registration records. He and his people probably bring in illegal aliens to stuff the ballot boxes."

"While Paul scams money off them," Scott finished. "They get 'em coming and going."

"I think we've got it figured," Nick said. "This is enough to pick up Krandall Senior *and* Junior for questioning."

"Can Elizabeth and I get an exclusive interview in exchange for our help?" Scott asked quickly.

Tom groaned. "Sinclair! Don't you ever give it a rest? Nick, you'll give me a statement, won't you?"

Nick knocked on the grate. "I'm not getting in the middle of this. This is between you guys and the chief." Nick knocked on the grate. "Jessica, let us out."

There was no response.

Elizabeth put her mouth close to the grate. "Jessica! We've figured everything out. Open the door."

"Maybe she can't hear us," Scott said.

Tom banged his fist on the wall. It made a resounding thump. It was answered by the grating rumble of a motor. The floor beneath Elizabeth's feet began to vibrate. "We're moving!" she exclaimed.

A sudden lurch of the van caused Elizabeth and everybody else to tumble to the floor.

"What's going on?" Scott demanded. "Your sister doesn't know how to drive something like this, does she?"

Heavy dread moved through Elizabeth's arms and legs, and her heartbeat slowed to a sickening thud. "No," she whispered fearfully. "She doesn't."

"Then someone else is out there," Tom croaked.

Chapter
Fifteen

What happened? Jessica's eyes fluttered open. The base of her skull ached with a dull throb. *Where am I? And what's all that noise?* She couldn't see a thing, and she felt as if her ears were pressed against a freight train.

She smelled the sharp, gassy odor of diesel fuel, and everything came rushing back. Someone had attacked her. *Paul Krandall* had attacked her, and then she had hit her head. How long had she been unconscious? It was impossible to know.

The engine grated harshly as gears shifted. They were going across rough terrain. Jessica jounced around on the floor. Her head bumped against the dashboard, sending sharp shock waves of pain through her cranium. But she made no noise. She didn't want to draw his attention to the fact that she was conscious.

Inside the dark mask Jessica pictured Elizabeth

and the others in the cargo area. They were probably being thrown around like rag dolls.

Not far from her head she could hear a foot stomping on the clutch and a hand clumsily shifting the gear. Paul's, she was sure. Driving this thing probably commanded his full attention.

She twisted her wrists. It was almost impossible to move them; the ropes were wrapped tightly around her bracelets.

The bracelets, however, weren't tight at all.

"Where is Paul?" Lila asked for about the fifteenth time.

"I really don't know," Anderson answered.

"He ran out behind Bruce, and I haven't seen him since," Pepper told her.

"How is my dress doing?" Lila asked, wrapping her VIP terry cloth robe more tightly around her.

Pepper got up off the couch and walked across the empty ballroom, where Lila's dress hung over the air-conditioning vent. "I'll see." Pepper felt the fabric, then examined the label. "What is this? Silk." She turned the tag over. "I don't recognize the name of this designer," she said as if she had just discovered a very serious flaw in Lila's character.

Lila would have said something snotty, but she wasn't too sure what her VIP standing was right now. And without Paul around she didn't really care either. She'd assumed that after she'd been fished out of the pool, he would come rushing in, tenderly take her hand, and ask her if she was all right after her ordeal. But she'd been waiting for over an hour now. Either he'd taken his father back to the motel or else he'd gone off in search of Bruce and his trophy.

I'm going to kill Bruce Patman, she thought. *He completely ruined what was shaping up to be the most important night of my life.*

Pepper came back and sat down across from her. "Your dress is still wet," she announced, studying Lila with a critical eye. "Who cuts your hair?" she asked.

"Billy, at La Hair," Lila answered promptly. Billy was the best-known hair stylist in town.

Pepper lifted her eyebrows, as if she were surprised. "Well," she said finally. "I guess there's only so much he can do with hair like that."

Lila gritted her teeth. "How wet *is* my dress?" she asked, deciding it was time to am-scray.

Anderson felt it. "Pretty wet," he announced. He began to laugh—that same high-pitched whinnying giggle. "I wish I had a video of you falling in the pool."

Pepper joined in the laughter. "When that dress floated out around you, you looked just like a frog sitting on a lily pad."

Anderson pointed at her. "Ribbit. Ribbit!" he croaked while Pepper shrieked and clapped.

"Ribbit! That's it. That's your nickname from now on." She pointed at Lila. "Ribbit! Ribbit!"

Lila's nostrils flared with anger. She really didn't

appreciate being told she looked like a frog. And they would call her *Ribbit* over her dead body. "That does it." She stood up and grabbed her purse. "I'm out of here."

"Where are you going?" Anderson asked.

"Home," she announced.

"You're leaving in a robe?" Pepper cried.

"No," Lila retorted. "This is what is known as *leaving in a huff*. When Paul comes back, tell him I can be reached at my dorm." She tugged the belt of her robe tighter, turned on her bare heels, and walked out of the ballroom.

"Ouch!" Elizabeth cried, rolling across the floor and banging her shoulder against the wall.

The transport vehicle bounced and jerked as it careened through the thicket. Low-hanging branches made reverberating thumps on the roof and walls. Rocks and roots flew up and banged against the floor and axle. Elizabeth could feel every one.

Something heavy rolled against Elizabeth. It was Tom. He wrapped his arm around her, cradling her head in the palm of his large hand. The van turned suddenly, and they both began sliding. Tom's hand protected her cheekbone from contact with the floor.

She heard cries of pain from Nick and Scott as they were thrown from one side of the compartment to the other. Their bodies made a sickening pounding noise as they collided and collapsed in a heap on the floor.

The ground leveled off, and Nick jumped to his feet and leaped toward the grate. His fingers curved over the tiny ledge and he held on while the van snaked for several moments.

When it leveled again, Nick anchored his body and extended his other hand. "Hang on to me," he shouted.

The van lurched, and Elizabeth and Tom rolled toward the back. Nick continued to hold on to the grate and extend his arm. Scott propelled himself from the back wall and jumped toward Nick's arm, grabbing it.

Elizabeth tried to get to her feet. Another violent lurch knocked her to the floor. This time the van tipped forward and she hurtled toward Nick and Scott. When they collided, Elizabeth threw her arms around Scott's waist. Tom came skidding behind her.

Elizabeth pressed her face into Scott's shoulder. His shirt was soaking wet with perspiration. Elizabeth realized she was soaking wet too. It was hot inside the van. Hot as the inside of an oven.

Jessica moved her wrists around one last time just to be sure the bracelets were as loose as she thought they were. She pulled her right hand slowly toward her body. Her elbow jammed against her stomach below her ribs. In this position she couldn't pull her hand through the bracelet.

She turned slightly sideways and waited.

Did Paul notice?

When his foot stomped on the clutch and his hand jerked the gearshift, she let out a silent breath of relief. His attention was still focused on driving. Jessica pulled her right hand out of the bracelet and flexed her fingers. *Ahhh! That feels good. When my chance comes, I'm ready to grab it.*

She tucked her chin and pushed the bag up just enough to see where the door handle was. Only inches away!

"Never underestimate the element of surprise," Nick had told her once.

Nick, this is for you, Jessica thought as she grabbed the door handle and came up from under the dashboard in one movement. The door opened, and she threw herself out into the bushes and brush. The impact was hard, and she rolled and rolled uncontrollably, but she couldn't have been happier.

She heard Paul shout something behind her, but she couldn't tell what it was. She snatched the bag from her head and took off, crouching low and trying to stay in the shadows.

The vehicle stopped with a screech of brakes. She heard Paul jump and trample through the brush behind her. Jessica lowered her head and ran faster. Thin branches whipped at her face, cutting at her cheeks.

Several yards below her she saw the road. With a cry of relief she started down the incline.

"One . . . two . . ."

When Tom said "three," Nick and Tom threw their shoulders against the door again. When the door didn't budge, they fell back, and Elizabeth and Scott stepped forward.

"One . . . two . . ." Elizabeth said "three," and this time she and Scott threw themselves at the door. It didn't budge. They positioned themselves for another assault, but Nick put his hand on Elizabeth's shoulder. "Stop. Stop. This is not going to work. These things are built to stay shut."

The floor shook slightly.

"Here we go again," Scott announced. He pulled Elizabeth toward him, and Nick saw Tom's face register annoyance. Nick reached for the grate again, but Tom put his hand there before Nick could. "Let me," he said grimly. "You may need that arm and hand. Don't wear it out."

Nick exhaled noisily. "You're right." He used his right hand to draw his gun—

His gun. He could shoot their way out of the van! He went for his holster and grabbed—

Nothing.

With a groan Nick realized that in the confusion before Jessica had shepherded them into the van, he'd dropped his gun. Dropped it and left it. Useless. Just like he was.

Nick pounded his head against the wall.

"Whoa," Tom said. "You might need that head too."

"No, I don't." Nick glowered. "I already lost it."

Tom raised an eyebrow and turned to Elizabeth.

"Liz, you hang on to me," Tom instructed. "Scott, you hang on to me and hold Nick."

The group arranged themselves as the vehicle lurched back into motion. There was a loud bang, a sickening dip, and then suddenly they were riding on a smooth surface.

"What happened?" Scott asked.

"We're on the road," Tom answered.

The road to where? Nick wondered.

Jessica popped up out of the ditch like a rabbit and watched the taillights of the van disappear around the curve of the road. Frantic, she got out on the road and began to run.

She looked behind her. No headlights. And no cars on the turnpike. Helpless and panicked, she began to shout. "Help! Help, somebody! *Help!*" The sound of her own frightened voice set off fresh waves of panic.

"Nick!" she shrieked. "Elizabeth!"

Reservoir Road coiled downward toward the reservoir, and she could see the red taillights appear and disappear as the cargo van continued down. "Nick!" she screamed again.

Jessica doubled over and clenched her fists in frustration. Paul was driving away with her sister and the man she loved, and there was nothing she could do.

She fell to her knees on the pavement and began to sob. "I should have stayed in the van!" she wailed, realizing she had made a horrible mistake. "I am *so stupid!"* She pounded her legs with her fists, choking on her tears.

A bright sheen of light fell over the pavement. She turned in time to see two bright headlights bearing down on her. Jessica jumped to her feet but held her ground. *"Stop!"* she screamed, holding out her hands and blocking the road so that the car had no choice but to obey.

The brakes squealed, and the car came to a skidding halt less than four inches from her body. She knew she looked like a maniac, so she stayed close to the car so the driver couldn't speed away without running over her. She clutched at the handle of the passenger door and pulled it open. "You've got to help me," she gasped. "Follow that van," she instructed, climbing into the front seat. "Hurry!"

Jessica wiped the tears from her eyes, took some deep breaths, then nearly fell out of her seat in surprise. *"Bruce!"*

Bruce Patman stared at her with large, frightened eyes. "Perdita?"

"No, it's me. Jessica."

Bruce continued to look confused.

"Jessica *Wakefield?"* she prompted.

His eyebrows practically disappeared into his hairline. "What . . . what . . . what are you doing out here? And why are you dressed up like Perdita del Mar?"

If Jessica hadn't been so frantic, she would have laughed. And Bruce thought *Paul* was slow on the uptake! "I'm not dressed up like Perdita del Mar," she explained. "I *am* Perdita. I mean, the person you think is Perdita is really me in disguise. I'm working undercover for the police."

Bruce snapped his fingers. "The police *are* investigating Paul's hustling scam. Right?" He smiled happily. "I *knew* it. I *knew* that guy was a crook. They probably ignored my report so they could lull in him into a false sense of security and catch him red-handed."

Jessica decided it was probably easier to agree. "You're absolutely right," she said. "But we've got to catch that van."

Bruce shook his head. "Can't be done. It's a dead end. The reservoir's down there, and they'll see us coming."

"OK, then, we'll get out and run." She started to get out of the car, but he locked the door and grinned.

"OK, then, we'll just go down with no lights."

"That's suicide!"

Bruce leaned over and opened the glove compartment. Jessica watched him press some buttons. Then he cut the lights on the car. "The McDougal Donner–designed computer-guided copilot system," he said with a smile. "It'll tell me if we're veering off the road."

With the lights off the dark seemed more vivid and frightening. Like a sea that might engulf them.

Bruce started forward, and Jessica clutched at the door. "Whatever happens," Bruce began, "I want you to promise me you'll tell Lila I actually used this thing. She was real snotty about it this afternoon."

"I promise," Jessica said softly as they wound their way slowly down Reservoir Road. She had no idea what would happen when they reached the bottom. But whatever happened, she would be with Nick and Elizabeth. For better or for worse. In sickness or in health. In life or . . .

Chapter Sixteen

"He left you in the pool to drown so he could go get his stupid trophy back?" Isabella stretched across Lila's bed and shook her head. "That guy *is* too dumb for words."

"I'm so glad you called us," Denise said, plopping down in Lila's desk chair. "It's times like these when you need your friends to cheer you up. Paul Krandall is a crumb bum. Forget him."

Lila leaned back against her Battenberg lace pillows. It was really humiliating that Paul never even came back to see if she was all right. "Maybe he went after Bruce to avenge me. He avenged Bunny," she said.

"That's possible," Isabella said. "But you know how guys are about trophies."

Lila felt slightly irritated that Isabella didn't immediately agree that Paul's disappearance had to do with *her* and not the trophy. A really good friend

189

would see how down in the dumps she was . . .

"If Paul doesn't call you tomorrow and ask for a date, can you get your campaign money back?" Isabella asked.

. . . and not rub it in. "I don't know," Lila answered miserably. "I hope so. I dropped two big contributions into that trophy."

"What if he doesn't ever call? Does that mean you won't get into the VIP Circle?" Denise asked, voicing Lila's biggest fear. "Yes," Lila answered. "And I'm not sure how much more cheering up I can stand from you guys."

"Sorry," Denise said. "Would it make you too unhappy if I asked how you left things with Bruce?"

Lila felt as if a lead weight had settled in her stomach. "I pretty much broke up with him."

Denise cleared her throat. "I hate to bum you out, but that probably wasn't the greatest move. If Paul doesn't call and you don't get into the VIP Circle, you—"

Don't have any boyfriend at all! Lila's mind screamed in a panic. "What have I done?" she moaned. "Bruce might not be perfect, but he's a great boyfriend."

"He *is* a great boyfriend," Isabella confirmed. "He cares about you a lot."

"He never forgets to call," Denise added.

Lila buried her face in her pillow, suddenly overcome with remorse. Tears began rolling down her cheeks. "Bruce will never speak to me again," she wailed. "How could I have been so stupid?"

"Bruce never stays mad for long," Isabella pointed out.

"This time it's different," Lila wept.

"You don't know that," Isabella argued. "Call him. Call him and see. He's probably back in his room, feeling like a total fool. He's probably just sitting there all by himself feeling sorry and lonely."

Lila reached for the phone and dialed. There was no answer. Bruce's answering machine clicked on and invited her to leave a message. "Bruce?" she said. "Bruce, it's Lila. Are you there? If you are, pick up."

She gave him more than enough time to get to the phone if he was within earshot. Was it possible he really didn't want to talk to her and make up?

Lila jumped up and reached for some slacks that were thrown across the back of her desk chair.

"What are you doing?" Isabella asked.

"Getting dressed. I'm going to find Bruce," she answered. "I've got to make sure he still loves me— and get him back."

"Silly!" Bruce exclaimed. "Lila said this was silly." He smiled a smile of deep satisfaction. It was nice to be so completely vindicated. Lila had acted like the possibility of needing a device like the McDougal Donner–designed computer-guided copilot system was ridiculous. *Ha! If she were here now, I'd make her eat*

191

those words like a watercress-and-arugula salad. He felt the wheels scrape against the rough shoulder. Automatically the car pulled left and back onto the road. "Did you feel that?" he asked Jessica. He couldn't have been prouder if he'd designed the McDougal Donner–designed computer-guided copilot system himself.

Jessica nodded but stared intently ahead. "What are you doing out here?" she asked.

Bruce reached into the back and held up the Verona Springs VIP Mixed Doubles trophy. "I'm going to throw this baby into the reservoir. And I hope Paul Krandall is there so he can watch me do it. I've been driving around thinking about it for a while. I almost chickened out and took it back to the club. But then I figured, hey, what can he do to me? Right?"

The thought of flinging Paul's stupid trophy into the reservoir made Bruce so happy, he almost forgot how angry he was at Lila. Maybe he should try and patch things up with Bunny. When you got past the size of those teeth, Bunny really had a very beautiful smile. He pictured himself walking into a restaurant with Bunny and seeing Lila and Paul. *Oops*. Make that Lila by herself. *"How's Paul?"* he would ask her, a lot of fake sympathy in his voice. Bunny would make some remark about how lucky she was to have broken up with him before he got sent to the clink. It would just kill Lila after all her talk about how wonderful the VIPs were if Paul turned out to be a convicted felon.

"How much jail time do you get for tennis hustling?" he asked Jessica.

"I don't really know," she answered vaguely.

"How can you *not* know when that's what the police want him for? Think he could get life?" He hummed happily at the prospect. "I guess not. That would just be too good to be true."

Jessica hesitated. "Actually, Bruce, that's possible. Because he might have killed somebody."

Bruce pounded the brake with his foot. The car came to a skidding stop, and the computer-guided steering system began to flash Copilot Deactivated . . . Copilot Deactivated . . . Copilot Deactivated in big, green, digital letters.

Bruce's good mood began evaporating like a shallow puddle in the afternoon sun. He could feel all that happiness clouding up and getting ready to dump back down on his head. "He *killed* somebody?"

Jessica nodded.

"Killed somebody as in *murdered* them."

Jessica nodded again.

"Somebody who beat him at tennis?" Bruce asked.

"No. Somebody else. I really don't know why. That's what we've been trying to find out."

"Who's *we?*" he asked. He snapped his fingers. "That's right. You're dating a policeman."

"Chip," Jessica confirmed.

"I thought his name was Nick."

"Nick is Chip."

Bruce's head began to hurt. He turned the key in the ignition and prepared to reverse.

"What are you doing?" Jessica cried.

"We're leaving," Bruce explained, trying to keep his voice calm. "I don't think it's a good idea to pursue a murderer down a dead-end road with a very deep body of water at the end of it."

Jessica leaned over and grabbed the wheel. "No! We can't go back!"

Bruce wondered if Lila had *any* friends who were sane. "The best thing to do is go back, call the police, and let *them* handle it. What can we do? We're just two college students, completely unarmed except for a tennis racket and a tin trophy cup. What am I supposed to do? Yell 'Freeze or I'll double fault'?"

It was like talking to a wall. Bruce could tell Jessica was just waiting for him to shut up so she could start arguing with him.

"There's no time. Elizabeth and Nick are in the van Paul is driving, and so are Scott Sinclair and Tom Watts. By the time we got back with the police, they could be dead."

"There's nothing we can do except go back to town and get help," Bruce said decisively. He reached toward the key again, but Jessica snatched it out of the ignition.

"Jessica!" he hollered. "Don't!" He lunged for her hand, but he wasn't fast enough. Jessica threw the key out the window. Then she pushed him away and opened the door, rolling out of the car and landing on her feet on the road. "Now we can't go back," she announced in a pleased tone. "We can only go forward."

Bruce sat perfectly still. He was as close to a complete nervous collapse as it was possible for a healthy nineteen-year-old male to be. *How does Nick . . . Chip . . . whoever . . . stand it?* he wondered. *How did Jessica's string of boyfriends cope?* There had been a lot of them. Maybe they had their own support group. If they didn't, they needed one. Jessica had just ruined Bruce's life, and he wasn't even dating her.

It sure made him appreciate Lila in a way he never had before. Lila was a little crazy when it came to social climbing. But so far she had never put him in a situation in which he was likely to be murdered—unless you counted the Verona Springs VIP Mixed Doubles Tournament.

He glanced at the trophy. Right now he would trade it—his McDougal Donner–designed computer-guided copilot system—and everything else he had just to be someplace else right now. Preferably someplace expensive. With Lila.

Jessica leaned into the car. "Come *on*," she urged.

Bruce shook his head. "No way. I'm not going. If you want to get killed, go ahead. I'm staying here. Sooner or later a car will come along, and I'll be able to go get the police."

"Bruce!" Jessica begged. "I can't go in there with no backup."

"Go ahead." Bruce handed her a tennis racket. "Make their day."

"Where do you think we are?" Tom asked, grateful for the smooth ride. The muscles in his shoulders and upper arms throbbed and ached. He squatted with his back against the wall and his feet against the floor.

"We're going downhill. And we're doing a lot of turning and twisting. So I'm guessing we're on Reservoir Road," Nick answered.

"I was afraid of that," Tom said, his stomach sinking. "The reservoir is where they found the body of the caddy."

"A reservoir is a good place to sink a body," Nick said. "And a cargo van," he added with ominous emphasis. "Did any of you tell anybody where you were going?"

"No. Normally I'd tell—" Tom broke off. Normally he would tell his partner, Elizabeth. But Elizabeth was Scott's partner now. "What about you guys?"

"Nobody knows where we are," Elizabeth answered tonelessly.

Nick shook his head in disbelief. "I can't believe you guys. How could you run off half-cocked like this? Don't you have any safety guidelines and procedures?"

"I'll draft some as soon as I get back to the station," Tom joked wryly.

Elizabeth laughed, but Scott looked slightly

sullen. Like he didn't want anybody telling him he was a jerk—even Nick. "Who knows where *you* are?" he asked.

"Jessica," Nick whispered.

"Big help now," Scott muttered.

Elizabeth sucked in her breath with a gasp, as did Nick and Tom. It was clear from the tone in Scott's voice that he considered Jessica dead—and furthermore, he was slightly irritated about it.

A stricken look crossed Elizabeth's face as if she hadn't yet considered the possibility. Tom's heart went out to her. He couldn't imagine how she was feeling now.

Yes, he could.

"I'm sure Jessica's fine," Tom said immediately.

Elizabeth's panicked eyes locked on his. In her face he saw a mute appeal for some kind of reassurance. He reached over and took her hands in his. "She's fine!" he repeated urgently. "You *know* she's fine."

Elizabeth's mouth trembled, and he tightened his grip on her hands.

Tom could hear Nick taking deep, hoarse breaths, as if he were trying not to lose it. "Jessica is *alive*," Tom insisted, determined not to let them lose heart. "Think how many scrapes she's been in and gotten out of. She's alert. She's on the ball. She probably saw whoever's driving this rig coming long before they saw her and hightailed it into town for help. Think about it! Do you really think she could be dead and you wouldn't know it, Liz?"

"You're right," Elizabeth said thickly. "She's like a cat. Only she's got ninety-nine lives." She smiled—a brave smile.

Nick sniffed and wiped his nose on the sleeve of his jacket. "She doesn't give up, I'll say that."

"No," Tom continued. "She doesn't. And neither should we."

"OK, OK," Nick interjected hoarsely. "You made your point. The sun'll come out tomorrow. Just *please* don't sing, OK?"

Tom laughed, and so did Elizabeth and Scott. Nick's humor broke the tension, and Tom could feel them take hope. Tom gave Elizabeth's hands a final squeeze and released them. "We need a plan. A strategy. When they open the door, we'll jump out and—"

"No," Nick argued. "We'd be like fish in a barrel. It would be too easy to shoot us. The best thing to do is stay calm and don't do anything to make whoever's out there pull the trigger. Wait for an opportunity."

"What if we don't get an opportunity?" Scott asked.

"There's always an opportunity," Nick answered. "You just have to be able to recognize it when you see it."

Chapter
Seventeen

"Just call me Indiana Joanie," Jessica quipped as she whacked at the brush with Bruce's tennis racket. Her arms and legs were exhausted from the long trek, but her eyes had gotten used to the dark. She could see the surface of the reservoir a quarter of a mile below. The transport was parked beside it.

Jessica tightened her grip on the racket and stopped. Now what? The adrenaline had long since drained away, and she was exhausted, winded, and hot.

Why didn't I let Bruce go for help? she wondered wildly. *What was I thinking? Where were my brains?* She swayed slightly, feeling woozy. She pressed her fingers experimentally against the back of her head where she had banged it on the dashboard. It was tender and wet. She examined the stain on her fingers. It looked black, but Jessica knew it was really red. She was bleeding.

Jessica rubbed the sticky blood off on the grass. Right now that was the least of her problems. The biggest problem was figuring out how to save her friends.

She squatted down, keeping her eye on the vehicle. Suddenly Jessica heard footsteps in the brush behind her. Her heart skipped a beat. *Somebody's out here in the dark with me!* Jessica threw herself forward and lay flat against the ground, pulling herself deep into the tangled foliage on her elbows.

She moved several yards forward and stopped, listening. The footsteps were getting closer. She scootched farther into the underbrush, then let out a shriek as a strong hand closed around her ankle and pulled her from her hiding place.

"Get ready to rock and roll," Elizabeth warned when she heard a clang somewhere outside. "Somebody's coming."

"Stay calm," Nick instructed.

Elizabeth looked at Tom and Scott. Everybody *was* calm. *Amazingly* calm, considering they'd been sitting here in agonized suspense waiting for their driver to make the next move.

Every passing second had been torture for Elizabeth. In spite of Tom's reassurances, she couldn't help worrying that Jessica was out there hurt and with no one to help her. No one to look for her.

Scott wiped his forehead on his sleeve.

Could Jessica really be dead? Cold, icy fear froze

the breath in her lungs. *No,* she thought, forcing herself to breathe. *If Jessica were dead, I'd feel it.* Jessica wasn't just Elizabeth's sister. She was her twin. An extension of Elizabeth's being. There was no way she could lose that part of herself and not know it.

The thought lifted Elizabeth's spirits. No matter what happened to her, maybe Jessica had a chance. She caught Tom's eyes watching her. She smiled sadly. He smiled back, and suddenly tears of regret welled up in her eyes. They had wasted so much time. *I love him,* she thought. *I've always loved him, and I always will. Why does it take the possibility of dying to make us realize what's important?*

She heard Nick and Scott's buzzing whispers as they discussed who and what might be on the other side of the doors. There was no way to talk to Tom without being overheard, but how could she *not* tell him how she really felt at a time like this? Why keep playing games?

Tom watched her with eyes that looked equally full of sorrow.

She moved toward him. "Tom."

His lips moved slightly, and then he reached for her, wrapping his arms and body around her, enveloping her. She hugged him as tightly as she could—feeling muscle and bone beneath his flesh.

There was so much that she needed to say. So much she wanted to hear. But time was running out. She could hear the clang and clatter of metal against metal. "Tom—"

His arms tightened around her. "Elizabeth—"

But there was no more time. They broke apart as the doors opened with a loud bang and metallic shriek.

Shaking with emotion, Tom tugged on Elizabeth's hand and pulled her down into a crouching position beside him.

Whatever happened now, he was ready for a fight. He'd held Elizabeth in his arms, and she'd returned his passion. If that wasn't a reason to live, he didn't know what was.

The cool night air worked on his nerves like a tonic. And he could see Elizabeth's eyes burning through the night like a cat's, waiting for her enemy to reveal itself.

He heard the crunching of boots and a tall figure appeared, walking around the back of the truck. He wore a black mask and held a pistol. "Get out," he said.

Nobody moved.

"Get *out*," the man repeated, gesturing with his gun.

"Paul?" Elizabeth ventured in a tentative tone.

Paul pulled the mask off his face and dropped it on the ground. "How did you know it was me?" He kept the gun trained on them and jerked it, signaling them to get out.

"They put two and two together and came up with four," Nick answered, hopping out of the van with his hands up. "They go to college, you know. Where's Jessica?"

"Who?"

"Perdita," Nick said impatiently. "Where is she?"

Paul shrugged. "I don't know."

Tom heaved a sigh of relief and heard Nick and Elizabeth both take long, shuddering breaths. If Paul didn't know, it meant Jessica was alive.

"Don't worry. We'll find her," Paul said as they hopped out of the back. "And she'll be found with the rest of you . . . at the bottom of the Verona Springs Reservoir." He shifted slightly. "Another tragic tale of teens and alcohol!"

"Who's *we?*" Tom asked. "You and your dad?"

Paul burst into hysterical giggles and pointed limply at Tom. "That's good. That's really, really good. You think this is, like, a father-son project?" He laughed even harder.

"Then who's Wil E. Coyote?" Nick asked.

Paul's laughter turned off, and his dull face turned sullen. "What makes you think it's not me?"

Nick didn't answer.

Paul's mouth twisted into an ugly sneer. "You don't think I'm smart enough?"

"Who is Wil E. Coyote?" Nick asked again. "And where is Manoel Coimbra?"

Paul's shoulders shook with contemptuous laughter. "You guys are about eighty-five percent there, but you *still* haven't got it figured out. Why does everybody think they're sooo *smart?* Why doesn't anybody want to give Paul credit for brains? That Mendoza kid, *he* thought he was a smart guy."

"He was smart enough to catch your mistake,"

Elizabeth said. "You were going over the list of deceased voters, pulling off the Hispanic names to use on phony papers, and didn't recognize one of them was Portuguese."

Paul popped his finger on his cheek and circled the air with it. "Smart guy, huh. I wonder how smart he feels now?"

"Was he trying to blackmail Coimbra?" Elizabeth asked.

"No. But Coimbra was scared anyway, so we sent him back to Mexico."

Elizabeth exchanged a glance with Tom. "But if Dwayne wasn't trying to blackmail him or you . . . why did you kill him?"

"We didn't mean to kill him. We meant to scare him into keeping his mouth shut. I didn't know he couldn't swim."

There was a distant crunch of boots on the gravel.

"Here's Wil E. Coyote now," Paul said. "It's show time."

Tom looked up and saw another masked man emerging from the brush. He'd obviously come from the opposite direction. He came to a surprised stop.

Shame and regret turned Tom's bones to rubber. In spite of the mask he knew immediately who the man was. It had been so obvious. How could he have missed it? Tom's stupid, naive willingness to trust him had signed their death warrants.

Who had access to voter records that yielded valuable information?

A congressman's son.

Who had access to willing workers who could be used as human cargo and ensnared in a web of blackmail and deceit?

A headwaiter at a country club with ties to Mexico.

Paul was an idiot, so that meant Carlos was the brains. As far as Carlos knew, Tom was the only member of the group with any certain knowledge of the scheme. Maybe if he kept his mouth shut and didn't identify Carlos, Carlos would go easy on them somehow.

But if he and Paul had been willing to kill Dwayne Mendoza just because he figured out one little clue, they would have no hesitation in killing a group of people who could put them behind bars for life.

Carlos turned to Paul. "I don't understand. Where is the driver? Where's the *freight*?"

"Change of plan," Paul answered. He nodded toward the group. "They'll have to go. We'd better sink the transport along with them," Paul said, almost conversationally. "Still haven't seen Bruce. I waited for him, but he probably wimped out." Paul laughed. "But keep an eye out for him. He'll have to go too." He lifted his gun and aimed it at Elizabeth, squinting down the barrel. "Might as well start with the little reporter lady."

"No!" Tom yelled. He heard his voice echoing across the reservoir as he dove toward Paul, prepared to throw himself in front of the bullet if he had to.

Paul swung his gun in Tom's direction just as Carlos's hand grabbed Paul's arm and shoved it upward, toward the sky. The gun discharged into the air.

Paul let out a yelp of surprise and backed off toward the brush, swinging his arm in an arc, keeping everybody, including Carlos, at bay. "What's the matter with you?" Paul demanded almost tearfully of his partner.

"Where are they?" Carlos asked Paul between clenched teeth. "Where are the people who were supposed to arrive tonight? They were supposed to be left here at the reservoir."

"They're in the hospital," Tom answered.

"*What?*" Carlos exclaimed.

"They were trapped in the back of that van all day. For hours. They're lucky to be alive," Elizabeth explained in a quavering voice.

Carlos's angry eyes turned toward Paul. "Is that true? You left them locked inside? A group that size? They could have died."

"I didn't have any choice." Paul's voice was defensive now. "They got here *way* ahead of schedule. They weren't supposed to be here until now, right? But they came in this morning. The driver thought he had a tail, so he split back toward the border. I stashed the van in a field until we could get back. But when I got back, the freight was gone. That Perdita chick was sitting in the cab, and these guys were locked in the back."

"You knew they were here all day and you didn't tell me! Why?"

Paul shrugged. "Because I knew you'd hock me to start getting them out, and it wasn't safe. Somebody might have seen them."

"OK. *Basta.* Enough. I'm *through* with this business, and I'm through with *you.*"

"What do you mean?" Paul demanded. "We're making more money than we ever dreamed."

Carlos shook his head. "You go too far for money. And you take me with you. No more."

Tom mentally reviewed what Paul had said earlier, noting the subtle shift in pronouns. *"We didn't mean to kill him. We meant to scare him into keeping his mouth shut. I didn't know he couldn't swim."*

Only *one* person was responsible for the murder. And it wasn't Carlos. "The people who were left in here could have died, but they didn't," Tom told Carlos. "*You* haven't murdered anybody yet. Don't make a bad situation worse."

"Don't listen to him," Paul argued.

"You guys brought Dwayne out here to beat him up," Tom persisted. "Then Paul threw him in the water and realized he couldn't swim. Is that what happened?"

"I wasn't here." Carlos groaned, his voice heavy with remorse. "I left. I didn't know he would throw him in the water after I had gone."

"That doesn't matter, Carlos," Paul yelled angrily. "Don't fall for it. We're partners, amigo. Fifty-fifty. You took fifty percent of the money. You take fifty percent of the blame."

"It doesn't work that way," a voice in the dark

said behind Paul. Before anybody could move, a large rabbit popped out of the bushes wielding a tennis racket and whacked Paul on the head with a loud *clonk*.

Tom momentarily thought he was hallucinating. But that was no rabbit. That was *Jessica!*

Paul swayed on his feet. Tom knew an opportunity when he saw one, and he dove again. This time Elizabeth dove with him. She hit Paul high and Tom hit him low. By the time they had him on the ground, Nick had Jessica in his arms. They embraced passionately.

Tom cleared his throat. "Uh, excuse me, Nick? I could use those handcuffs now."

"Get into the van," Carlos ordered roughly.

Tom's stomach clenched when he looked up and saw Carlos holding them at gunpoint.

"Get in the van," Carlos ordered again.

"You're not a killer," Tom said, his heart pounding mercilessly. "I *know* you, Carlos. You're not."

"No. But I'm not going happily to jail." Carlos motioned with the gun. "Into the van. You'll go with me as hostages."

Tom held out his hand. "Give me the gun."

Carlos shook his head, backing up. "No. Stay back."

Tom continued toward him.

"Tom," Nick bellowed. "Get away."

Tom stared unflinchingly into Carlos's eyes. *"Give me the gun,"* he urged.

"Get back!" Carlos screamed, his voice rising in

panic. His hand began to shake, and he cocked the revolver.

The click echoed in Tom's brain like a thunderclap. But he wasn't going to back down. He stepped forward again, holding his breath.

Carlos stood, his hand shaking. After what felt like an eternity, he threw the gun down, turned, and ran.

Another figure shot up out of the tangle of bushes and whacked Carlos on the head with a big silver trophy cup. He dropped to the ground, groaning.

At that very moment a gleam of headlights swept around the corner of the road and illuminated the scene. Tom froze, squinting into the glare. Was it the police? More of Paul and Carlos's band of smugglers? He reached out and felt Elizabeth tuck her hand into his.

"Bruce!" a familiar voice cried.

Tom heard a door open, and the next thing he knew, Lila Fowler was running toward them through the haze of the headlights.

"Lila!" Bruce stepped into the light, dropped the trophy cup, and opened his arms. Lila threw herself into them, and he folded her against his chest.

Tom looked at Elizabeth. She appeared as amazed as he felt. Then they began to smile.

Nick was closing the cuffs over Paul's wrists. He stood up and walked over to where Tom stood over Carlos, picking up guns and starting the routine work of securing a crime scene.

Tom watched Elizabeth's smile begin to tremble. He turned her discreetly away and put his arms around her. Neither one of them said a word. She sagged against him, expelling her breath in a long, quaking sob.

"Elizabeth, Elizabeth," he soothed, stroking the top of her hair.

Her arms reached around and circled his waist. "Promise you'll never do anything like that again," she wept. "Promise!"

"I can't promise that," he whispered. "Nobody's going to hurt you. Not as long as I'm around to stop them."

Elizabeth relaxed in his embrace, then turned her face up toward his. Their lips were inches apart, growing closer.

"Elizabeth!" Jessica shrieked, pulling Elizabeth from his arms.

Their moment was over. The magic spell that had briefly enveloped them was broken, and the quiet reservoir was suddenly a hive of activity.

Jessica and Elizabeth talked, laughed, and cried at the same time. Pretty soon Lila and Bruce were trading stories. Nick got on Lila's cell phone and telephoned for backup. Scott found a pad in the back of Lila's car and began scribbling notes. Within minutes a police chopper was circling overhead. The lights burned down on the reservoir. The surface rippled in the wind of the chopper blades. Sirens pierced the air, announcing the approach of police cars.

By the time they arrived, Elizabeth's embrace felt like a distant memory. Tom wasn't completely sure it had really happened. And if it had, he had no idea what it meant.

As policemen arrived and began asking questions and taking statements, Elizabeth became more and more composed. More and more distant. She and Scott stood side by side, nodding and explaining as a detective jotted down their story.

Elizabeth glanced over her shoulder, nodding toward the van, obviously describing the scene. As she talked and pointed, her eyes flickered past Tom—registering no emotion whatsoever.

Tom swallowed and looked down at the toes of his boots, trying not to cry. OK. It had been one of those near-death-experience things. What did he think? That he was going to mumble a few words, kiss her, and make the whole lousy past disappear?

Grow up, he told himself angrily. *Just grow up already.*

Elizabeth sat in the back of Nick's car between Tom and Scott. Jessica sat in front with Nick, her head resting on his shoulder. "Who wants to be dropped where?" he asked as he turned onto the main road leading to the SVU campus.

"I want to go to the station," Tom said.

Elizabeth felt Scott nudge her. She knew he was worried that Tom was going to beat them to the public with the story. But Elizabeth wasn't worried. Television news was immediate and informational. But she knew that she could do more with this story in print than she could on tape. There would be enough interest in what had happened to keep the station and the paper busy for a long time.

Tom directed Nick to the station, and the car stopped. Tom reached across Elizabeth and extended his hand to Scott. "You did a good job out there tonight."

Scott hesitated a moment before returning Tom's handshake. "You too," he said.

Elizabeth wished Scott could seem less grudging. His reluctance to shake Tom's hand and return the compliment made him seem small. And kind of petty.

When Tom got out, he turned and leaned in, taking Elizabeth's hand. He shook it. "Good night," he said. "You were terrific."

Elizabeth waited for him to say something more personal. More intimate. But he seemed hesitant. Maybe because Scott was in the car. "Tom," she began, breaking off when she saw Dana Upshaw come running out of the station door.

"Tom!" Dana shrieked as if she had been waiting for him to return from World War II. The moment Tom turned around, Dana threw herself at him. "I heard on the radio that a WSVU reporter had been involved in a shoot-out at some reservoir." Her eyes were red and swollen, and her cheeks were tear-stained. "I've been frantic."

"No. No," he soothed, hugging her and kissing the top of her head. "It was nothing like that. I'm fine. Everybody's fine."

His voice was soft and reassuring. *Just like it was with me,* Elizabeth thought, feeling as if she had been slapped. Whatever had passed between them at the reservoir had been generic hero-comforts-damsel-in-post-traumatic-distress. Nothing personal. Nothing real. Nothing true.

Tom gave Elizabeth and Scott a wry smile. "I guess I'd better start putting together the story. The sooner I get on the air with the truth, the sooner the wild rumors will stop circulating. G'night."

As he walked up the pavement with his arm around Dana, Elizabeth felt her throat quivering. Was she ever going to learn to let go?

"I want to get started on this story right away," Scott told her as Nick pulled away from the curb and proceeded on to Dickenson Hall. "Let's try to get an edition out by next Monday. That'll give us time to get all the information, all the facts, and put together the fullest and most complete account of what happened."

Jessica turned around in the seat and rolled her eyes. "Don't you guys ever just, you know, *relax?*"

That got a laugh out of Scott. He smiled apologetically at Elizabeth. "Way uncool," he conceded. "Take a shower. Have something to eat. *Then* meet me back at the newspaper office."

Nick stopped the car, and Elizabeth opened the door. "I'll see you in a couple of hours."

Jessica kissed Nick good-bye. An embarrassingly long, passionate, steamy kiss. Elizabeth stifled a giggle. She knew Scott was probably looking at his watch, trying to figure out how much longer this was going to take.

Finally Jessica removed herself from Nick's arms. "What time will you be through at the station?" she asked.

"I'll probably be there till morning," he answered. "Want me to pick you up for breakfast?"

Jessica climbed out and pulled the clips out of her hair, letting it fall around her shoulders. "Better make it lunch. I'm going to try to score a hair appointment in the morning. Get back to the blond."

"All right," Nick said softly before driving away with Scott.

Elizabeth tilted back her head and gazed up at the night sky. "It's incredible how much stuff happened in a short amount of time," she said with a laugh.

"More than you could ever guess," Jessica commented quietly.

Elizabeth studied Jessica's face. It was different. It wasn't just the makeup, hair, and brows. Something had changed. Something *inside* Jessica.

"Let's go upstairs," Elizabeth said, pulling Jessica toward the dorm. "We've got a *lot* to talk about."

"Let me be sure I have this one hundred percent straight," Bruce said. Sometimes Lila skipped tracks so fast, he had a hard time keeping up. "Becoming a Verona Springs VIP is no longer a goal?"

"Not a goal," Lila confirmed, settling herself more comfortably in the crook of his arm.

"We don't have to go back there ever again?"

"I wouldn't be caught dead in a dump like that," Lila responded.

Bruce sighed contentedly.

"You were so brave," Lila breathed, her voice awed. "I still can't believe you actually left your Porsche on the side of the road to go off after Jessica."

Bruce had a hard time believing he'd actually done it too. As soon as Jessica had disappeared into the night, he'd realized he couldn't sit there and let her get killed. It was against the Geneva code or something. He'd pursued her all the way down Reservoir Road, determined to bring her back.

He'd been afraid to call her name for fear of being overheard, but unable to quite catch up with her until he'd managed to grab her by the ankle. By then the whole scene was in full gear, and there was no way to back out. They could only—as Jessica happily pointed out—go forward.

"This is a whole new side of you." Lila shivered. "I had no idea you were so heroic. So impulsive. So dynamic and forceful. And I still can't believe you left your car unattended by the side of the road."

"Me either. Those McDougal Donner–designed computer-guided copilot systems are a cinch to steal.

And just in case you don't think that came in handy—"

"Let's not talk about it," Lila said quickly, cutting him off by pressing her lips hungrily against his.

"It's unclear at this time whether or not Congressman Krandall had any direct knowledge of his son's activities," Tom reported, "but WSVU will keep you informed as this story develops. This is Tom Watts. Good night."

Scott pressed the mute button and swiveled around in his chair to face Elizabeth. "He did a good story."

Elizabeth continued to stare at the screen. The campus news was repeated every hour. Between the broadcasts the station ran trailers. Clips of old and new pieces.

She saw film of herself. Film of Tom. Film of the two of them running toward a fire. They had covered a lot of stories together and savored a lot of triumphant moments.

It felt weird not to be sharing this one with him.

"Hey!" A hand passed back and forth in front of her eyes.

Elizabeth forced her attention away from the television. Scott swiveled thoughtfully in his chair. He'd showered and changed, and his hair was still slightly damp and combed straight back. His blue eyes were tired, but they burned with an unrelenting enthusiasm that Elizabeth recognized and respected.

"Where were you?" he asked gently. He scooted

his desk chair closer to hers and brushed a strand of her freshly shampooed hair from her shoulder.

"I was someplace else," she said, having no good answer.

He leaned forward, and Elizabeth closed her eyes. "Where?" he whispered, his breath warm and sweet on her face.

Elizabeth had no response to that either. She could only think about what was about to happen. Why fight it? The sooner they got it over with, the sooner she could remind him she wasn't interested. That she could *never* be interested.

She felt his fingers trace the contours of her face fleetingly, gently, as if she were being kissed by the wind. It felt nice, she had to admit. Soothing. Comfortable. His lips brushed against hers quickly, then nothing, as if he were waiting for her to recoil and push him away as she had done so many times before.

She didn't.

She wanted more.

His lips pressed against hers softly, lingeringly; she let her own lips meet his kiss for kiss, and when she smiled, she sensed he was smiling too. His hand buried itself in her hair, the passion in his kisses building. She didn't pull away, instead reaching up and caressing his cheek. It was freshly shaven. Smooth and cool. He smelled good. He felt good. He felt . . . *right*?

She moved her hand to the back of his neck and pulled his head closer, not wanting to stop, not wanting to come up for air. When they broke apart, she kept her eyes closed, unwilling to open them to reality.

"Elizabeth?" Scott asked hesitantly, his hand still lingering in her hair. "Liz . . . are you OK . . . with this?"

She opened her eyes slowly. Part of her had been hoping to see someone other than Scott sitting before her. But to her surprise, the realization that she had been kissing Scott wasn't quite as shocking as she expected. But somewhere in the back of her mind, she was still connecting his lips to someone else's face. "I don't know," she said truthfully.

Scott's blue eyes flickered, and he let out a sigh—of disappointment or relief, Elizabeth couldn't tell. Letting her hair fall through his fingers like sand, he leaned forward and took both of her hands in his. "Elizabeth, I need to tell you something."

She lifted her eyes. "What?"

"I might be going away."

She closed her eyes and felt slightly relieved. No matter how good a kisser Scott was, she wasn't ready for a new romance. If he left, she would be spared the trouble of sorting out a lot of very confusing feelings.

"Where are you going?" she asked.

He let go of her hand and took a manila envelope from the in-box on the desk they shared. "I've applied to the Denver Center for Investigative Reporting. In Colorado."

Elizabeth had heard of it. The place was unbelievably prestigious. You had to be a stellar journalist to even be considered. And if you got in, you were guaranteed not only the best education and Pulitzer Prize–winning professors but also the job of your choice when you graduated.

"I think you ought to apply too," Scott told her. "You could win a scholarship."

Elizabeth pushed away, the castors beneath her chair squeaking in protest. "I couldn't. There's no way . . ."

Scott grasped the back of her chair and pulled it back toward him. "Why not?"

"I couldn't get in," she said.

"You will after you write this story," he responded. He put the envelope in her hand. "Think about it."

Elizabeth rolled her chair slowly over to her desk. She put the envelope in the top drawer and turned on her PC. If, by some miracle, she actually won a scholarship, it would mean leaving SVU. Leaving *Tom*.

On the other hand, maybe that wasn't such a terrible thing.

Chapter
Eighteen

"So Carlos had nothing to do with the murder?" Isabella asked, lowering the newspaper and putting her feet up on the Thetas' rickety old parlor-room coffee table.

"No. He won't be facing murder charges," Jessica said. "But he's still in a lot of trouble. And there were scads of other people involved. Drivers. People who made phony IDs. And those are just the people they've found in the last few *days!* Nick says they'll be making a ton of arrests over the next month or so. It's a huge ring."

Lila twisted her hair into a knot and then let it fall with a laugh. "When you were dressed like Perdita, I kept wondering who you reminded me of. I still can't believe all that was happening and you didn't tell me."

"I couldn't tell you what was going on even if I wanted to," Jessica said. "For one thing, I didn't know everything myself. I had to read it in the paper today just like you guys. Like the part about the money and Tom's ten-dollar bill."

"It's like a novel or something," Denise said. "I can't believe it. I had to go all over campus to find a copy of the boring old *Sweet Valley Gazette*. I finally had to dig one out of the garbage at the library."

"Eeew!" Lila groaned.

Denise rolled her eyes. "It was in the *recycling bin*, silly."

"Still, it was a *used* newspaper," Lila insisted. "Who *knows* where that thing's been, Denise?"

Jessica's copy was folded in her lap. The story took up the entire issue. Elizabeth had gotten interviews with lots of the people involved—including Jessica. She was prouder than proud. But her heart ached when she saw the picture of the cargo van interior—the cramped prison in which all those helpless people had gasped for air and water in the sweltering heat.

In all the excitement of the aftermath, she didn't want to forget that this had involved real lives and real people. People like the young man who had taken her hand and asked for her help. She knew his name now: Pedro Cruz. And this hadn't been his first attempt to live and work in the United States. He'd worked at the country club as a busboy. Using the name *Manoel Coimbra*.

As soon as Nick discovered that, Pedro had become a very important witness for the prosecution.

That meant they needed him to stay while they prepared the case. Nick said that given the size of the case and the slowness with which the judicial system moved, Pedro would probably be eligible for citizenship by the time it was over. Jessica hoped so. She hoped that there would be a happy ending for everyone who deserved it—including her and Nick.

She looked at her watch. She was supposed to meet him at the diner soon. He'd been busy for several days with the arrest reports, and they hadn't had much time together.

Jessica held up a lock of her hair and inspected the ends. "I never dreamed it was going to be so hard to get all that dye out of my hair. It was just supposed to be *semipermanent*, right? But I've been to the salon twice, and look—I can still see some of it."

"If you had known, would you have taken a pass on the adventure?" Isabella asked teasingly.

Jessica dropped her hair and giggled. "Not in a million years!"

Elizabeth thanked the caller and put down the telephone. The *Gazette* phone she shared with Scott had been ringing nonstop all morning with people calling and offering congratulations on the story. And it was only Monday. The paper had only been out for a matter of hours!

Absently she looked over her application for the Irving Tindell scholarship. Scott had urged her to fill it out, and she had. But she felt shy about sending it in. Shy about holding her work up for comparison with some of the best and the brightest in the country.

"Elizabeth!" she heard a voice call.

She looked up and smiled. "Brandon Phillips?"

Brandon stood awkwardly at her desk with a square gift-wrapped package in his hand. "I wasn't sure you'd recognize me without my orange jumpsuit."

"You look better without it." She stood up and pretended to look him up and down. "Yep. I think this look is a lot better."

Brandon laughed and looked down at his jeans and boots. His hair was styled, and his prison pallor was almost gone. "I came by to thank you. You and Scott." He looked around.

"He's at the university center, but I'll tell him you came by."

Suddenly Brandon seemed to remember he had a gift. He thrust it toward Elizabeth. "Here. I didn't know what to get you guys, so . . ." He shrugged. "It's dumb. I'm sure you already have one, but . . ."

Elizabeth tore off the paper and let out a delighted cry. "A dictionary!" He was right. They *did* have a dictionary. But she didn't care. "I love dictionaries," she said truthfully. She put it on the desk and arranged her mug against it like a bookend. "There. I think it's happy there. But the best present is seeing you out from behind bars."

"They let me out that very night. I owe you and Scott big apologies. If it weren't for you, I might have spent my whole life in jail. Thank you. Thank you for caring about the truth." He lifted his hand in a farewell gesture and left quickly.

His simple words and straightforward feelings touched Elizabeth's heart. Caring about the truth. That's what journalism was supposed to be. She cared about the truth, and the truth had set Brandon Phillips free.

Elizabeth dropped her eyes to the desk. She ran her eyes over the application form one more time. She no longer felt shy about showing her work. She was proud of it. Very proud.

But she still wasn't sure she wanted to leave Sweet Valley University and all its memories behind.

Tom sat in the cafeteria and drained his coffee cup as he read the last of Elizabeth's story. Man! Could she write or what?

He looked at the reproduction of the postcard she had received just before going to press and laughed out loud. Trust Elizabeth to scoop him.

Dear SVU Reporters,
I have heard from relatives in Sweet Valley that you feared for my safety. I am happy to report that I am alive and enjoying a vacation in my native country of Guatemala. Thank you for righting a great wrong. I will be returning home soon and will thank you in person. I am looking forward to

my retirement after many years of work and will be living with my grandson, Dr. Felix Mendoza. He is a professor of neurology at Sweet Valley University. His address is enclosed. Until then I remain,

Yours gratefully,
Juan Mendoza

Juan Mendoza. The missing gardener. Not the victim of foul play after all. The last loose end was tied up, and Elizabeth had managed to make a human story out of a thorny social issue and human beings out of the villains without sugar coating.

Elizabeth's article made him realize he hadn't been all wrong in his assessment of Carlos. Carlos was a decent man who had momentarily lost his way. He'd started out smuggling in his relatives to help them. Then he'd met Paul. Paul had provided the money for a van and access to information that could be used to fabricate IDs.

The income from the first "haul" had provided enough money for a second van. The second "haul" produced more income. The next thing Carlos knew, he was the brains behind a huge and very successful business. An *illegal* business. He'd been looking for the American Dream and found the American Nightmare.

Tom made a note to go see him in jail. Maybe he could help him. Carlos was a bright man. And a good man. Who knew? The second time around he might get it right.

Out the window he saw Elizabeth walking across the quadrangle, hugging a manila envelope against her chest. They'd hardly spoken since the night of the arrests. He'd gone out of his way to stay too busy to drop by or call. He was afraid of being turned away again. He remembered the way her body had leaned into his after he had confronted Carlos. The emotion that had shaken her voice echoed in his ears. He'd thought about that moment constantly. Analyzed it over and over. She'd cared about him then. He knew that.

What were her feelings now?

It would have been easy to turn his attention back to the newspaper. To pretend he hadn't seen her. But he'd been a coward long enough. Tom stood up and hurried out of the cafeteria.

"No, no. Sit here." Nick tugged on Jessica's hand, pulling her into the booth beside him. He put his hand on her head and gently led it to his shoulder.

They were in the diner, and Nick had just come from the station after a twenty-four-hour shift. He looked tired and haggard, but he was in a good mood. "I want you to pretend something with me," he said.

Jessica giggled, feeling silly sitting in the middle of a diner in broad daylight with her head on Nick's shoulder.

"Close your eyes," he said sternly. "You can't pretend with your eyes open."

She closed her eyes, then peeped to see if his were closed too. They were. He leaned his head back on the plastic upholstery. "I want us to pretend we're at the Old Maple Steak House."

"Never heard of it," she said.

He lifted his head and opened his eyes wide. "You're kidding. I never took you there?"

Jessica sat up. "Do you think you did?"

Nick's face turned wary. He was thinking. She could see him going down the list of women he had taken there. He obviously realized she wasn't on it. "We'll go Saturday night," he said.

She fixed him with a tough girl squint. "Maybe we will. Maybe we won't. It pretty much depends on you."

He sat up and removed his arm, hearing the message in her joke. "OK. What's on your mind?"

"Did . . . did you mean the things you said about my instincts being good and all that?"

His face immediately closed. "Yes. But I know what you're going to ask, and the answer is no. You can't go with me again. Not ever. I just can't worry about you like that. I . . ." He swallowed. "I . . ." He swallowed again. His rugged face lost its tough veneer, and his eyes turned vulnerable. He looked ashamed. "I love you."

They were beautiful words. Not long ago just hearing them made Jessica's life feel complete. But she was different now. And she had a goal beyond just being loved.

"I want to leave school," she said, figuring the

sooner she got it out there, the sooner they could deal with it. "I want to leave school and go to the Police Academy."

"What a coincidence." He pinched the bridge of his nose. "Because I want to leave the police force and go to college. Prelaw."

"Is that a joke?" she gasped.

"Nope."

The waitress appeared with two rattling coffee cups and placed them on the table. Her shoes squeaked on the floor as she briskly retrieved the coffeepot from behind the counter.

Jessica forced her hands to be still in her lap. "I don't know what to say."

Nick picked up his spoon and began stirring his coffee. "I'd say we've got a problem."

"Kudos and congratulations!" Tom waved the paper triumphantly.

Elizabeth felt her throat and cheeks flush. She was glad to see Tom going out of his way to flag her down. She'd thought he was avoiding her. That he was embarrassed by the way she acted that night because he didn't feel about her the same way she felt about him.

"Great story," he said, tapping the newspaper against his thigh. "I had to tell you."

"I've been watching you on the news," she responded. "Your coverage has been great."

He accepted the compliment with a tight smile followed by an awkward silence. "It's real different being a solo act," he said. Elizabeth frowned. Did he mean different-bad? Or different-good? Or was he telling her he was capable of following a story by himself and didn't need a partner?

He opened the paper and pointed to a couple of shared bylines. "Must be nice having somebody to help."

"Are you saying that you don't think I could have written this without Scott's help?"

"No!"

"Are you saying I couldn't have gotten the story without Scott's help?"

Tom looked left and right, like he couldn't figure out why she was asking such an obvious question. "Well . . . you couldn't have. Neither could I. Neither could he. We all helped each other get the story."

"Oh." Elizabeth cleared her throat and looked away.

The silence grew longer and deeper. Finally Tom slapped the paper against his thigh. "So, good work and I'll see you around." He turned his back and walked quickly back toward the university center.

Elizabeth watched his back with her lip trembling. Maybe it was time to leave Sweet Valley University *and* her memories. Tom was her past. Her career was her future. It was time to quit clinging to her security blanket. Time to take that big leap forward.

She heard her tears falling on the manila envelope in her hand. They slightly smudged the address. She took one last look at Tom's retreating back, as if it would give her some kind of sign to stop what she was about to do. Finding no such sign, she took one last look at the envelope containing her application to the Denver Center for Investigative Reporting before she jammed it into the nearest mailbox.

Tom Watts is on the verge of breaking through to Elizabeth Wakefield—but one false move could send her into Scott Sinclair's arms for good. What will Tom do next? Find out in Sweet Valley University #36, HAVE YOU HEARD ABOUT ELIZABETH? Coming to bookstores in February. In the meantime don't miss this new, blood-chilling SVU Super Thriller:

Nina Harper and Bryan Nelson have become guinea pigs in a bizarre on-campus science experiment. They thought they'd be earning fast cash, but they may end up paying with their lives! Can Elizabeth Wakefield help expose the deadly truth before it's too late? Find out in the next Sweet Valley University Thriller Edition, CHANNEL X.

SIGN UP FOR THE SWEET VALLEY HIGH® FAN CLUB!

Hey, girls! Get all the gossip on Sweet Valley High's® most popular teenagers when you join our fantastic Fan Club! As a member, you'll get all of this really cool stuff:

- Membership Card with your own personal Fan Club ID number
- A Sweet Valley High® Secret Treasure Box
- Sweet Valley High® Stationery
- Official Fan Club Pencil (for secret note writing!)
- Three Bookmarks
- A "Members Only" Door Hanger
- Two Skeins of J. & P. Coats® Embroidery Floss with flower barrette instruction leaflet
- Two editions of *The Oracle* newsletter
- Plus exclusive Sweet Valley High® product offers, special savings, contests, and much more!

Be the first to find out what Jessica & Elizabeth Wakefield are up to by joining the Sweet Valley High® Fan Club for the one-year membership fee of only $6.25 each for U.S. residents, $8.25 for Canadian residents (U.S. currency). Includes shipping & handling.

Send a check or money order (do not send cash) made payable to "Sweet Valley High® Fan Club" along with this form to:

SWEET VALLEY HIGH® FAN CLUB, BOX 3919-B, SCHAUMBURG, IL 60168-3919

NAME_____
    (Please print clearly)

ADDRESS_____

CITY_____ STATE_____ ZIP_____
                                                  (Required)

AGE_____ BIRTHDAY_____ /_____ /_____

Offer good while supplies last. Allow 6-8 weeks after check clearance for delivery. Addresses without ZIP codes cannot be honored. Offer good in USA & Canada only. Void where prohibited by law.
©1993 by Francine Pascal   LCI-1383-123